BEACHED IN BALI

Beached IN BALI

BEACHED IN BALI

Island Escapes Series

ERIN BROCKUS

GREEN SAGE PRESS

Edited by Lawrence Editing Services

Cover design by GetCovers ———

Ebook ISBN: 978-1-957003-21-4

Paperback ISBN: 978-1-957003-22-1

Chapter One

Dawn

"LADIES AND GENTLEMEN, we are initiating our descent into Denpasar. Flight attendants, please prepare the cabin for landing."

The pilot's announcement and the motion of the 777 edging downward woke me from my stupor. I glanced out the window beside me. Nope, still only white clouds and blue ocean below, with an occasional island to break up the image.

We'd been flying forever. At least it felt that way.

But we're almost there. Finally!

I turned my head toward a soft murmuring from my right. Cole Foster, my best friend and current glutton for punishment, was asleep with one long leg stretched into the aisle. I glanced at the leg in question. Poor guy. I'd upgraded our flights to premium economy at the check-in counter. A little extra legroom was the least I could do for my six-foot-four wingman.

I nudged him with my elbow. "Cole! Wake up. We're descending."

Blinking his hazel eyes open, he glanced at me blearily. "Huh? What's wrong?"

"Nothing's wrong. We're almost in Bali!"

Cole rubbed his eyes and straightened in his seat, drawing his leg back into the area allotted for it. I winced and tried not to imagine blood clots flying loose as he adjusted his position, trying to keep his knees from contacting the seat in front of him.

"Thank God," he said, squinting out the window. "I hope I can still walk."

"If not, I promise to get you one of those escort carts with the flashing light." I grinned as he shot me a dirty look. He attempted to smooth his rumpled, light-brown hair. Normally, he kept it neatly combed, but now it was flattened on one side where he'd leaned against the headrest.

Our first flight from LAX to Singapore had been over fifteen hours. By comparison, the less than three-hour flight from Singapore to Bali should have been a breeze.

At least that's what I kept telling myself.

Cole had paced the aisles every few hours to ensure the circulation in his legs didn't shut off. I couldn't help but smile as he returned the sympathetic nods and smiles from passengers commenting on how uncomfortable he must be.

Being of average height myself, I was under no delusions this seemingly endless series of flights was much harder on him. Which was another reason I was so grateful to have him here.

"How long is the drive to the resort?" he asked.

"Two and a half hours."

Cole groaned. "Why did I agree to this?"

"Because you can't resist helping a friend in need. It's part of your DNA."

"I need a DNA transplant." He blinked his bloodshot eyes. "How many days have we been flying? I feel like my brain doesn't even work anymore."

"Yeah. I know what you mean. Today is Sunday. I think we left Los Angeles on Friday."

Two months prior, a vacation to Bali had been my idea. A chance to fulfill my childhood dream, when I'd watched a kid's program about the *Magical World of Bali* and gotten hooked on the destination. And a chance to jolt myself out of the dull status quo I'd let myself slip into. Though fully prepared for a solo vacation, Cole had flat-out refused to let me go by myself when I explained my plans.

"Dawn, I'm not letting you traipse halfway around the world all alone," he'd said, crossing his arms over his broad chest as we stood in the kitchen of my small apartment.

"I'm twenty-five, Scarecrow, not some kid. I can handle myself."

I'd hoped to win him over by using the nickname I'd given him years ago, but it didn't work. Sympathy flickered in his eyes for a moment before he covered the expression. "I know you can. I also know you've been through hell the past year and you shouldn't be alone for this trip. I can get some vacation time at the gym." Then he pointed at me. "I'm going. End of story."

Despite my bravado, I'd been relieved at his declaration. My life was nothing like I'd imagined when younger. I was floundering and without identity. When a seven-night trip to Bali with airfare had appeared on a travel deal website I subscribed to, it had to be fate. The trip was an attempt to reconnect with my younger self—to figure out who I was and wanted to be.

But that didn't mean I wanted to be alone.

And Cole was more travel-wise than me. His swimming career had seen to that. One year older, he'd moved home to San Bernadino six months ago to take over a gym whose owner was retiring. I'd never been out of the United States. The last time I'd been on a plane was two years prior. To support Cole—my best friend. That had been the beginning of the end of my marriage to Blake. And the start of my aimless, wounded identity.

With anticipation building, I stared out the window the entire landing, occasionally moving to let Cole have a look. The first things I deciphered of the Island of the Gods as we descended were turquoise water and a bustling, packed town. Then misty emerald peaks appeared, dominating the interior of the island. Then the plane landed smoothly and taxied to the terminal.

Cole had studied the immigration process, but between our combined brain fog, it took much longer than expected. But eventually, Cole and I made it through immigration and collected our two suitcases. As we walked toward the frosted glass Exit doors with the other arrivals, the modern, air-conditioned terminal hummed with quiet excitement.

"Someone is supposed to pick us up, right?" Cole asked.

"Yes. I got confirmation a driver will be waiting, and holding a sign with my name on it. I'm sure we'll be able to pick him out."

As we walked side by side, the doors opened before us.

Loud, shouting chaos replaced the quiet hall as we stepped through. A long rope cordon separated us from a throng of people on the other side. Stuffed cheek by jowl, men and women held signs and shouted, trying to get the arriving passengers' attention. We were still inside, but after the relative quiet of the immigration area, this was a jarring, intimidating mess.

"My God," I breathed, a deep disquiet rolling through my stomach. I glanced at Cole, grateful for his height. "Can you pick him out?"

Cole barked a laugh. "I can't see anything but a mass of people. Let's be systematic and start at the left. We'll work our way right."

I tried to take comfort from his confidence. The noise in the hall was deafening as passengers shouted to get drivers' attention and vice versa. I blinked, trying to concentrate with my fuzzy, muddled mind. As I combed the sea of signs without seeing my name, frustration mounted. We moved methodically, but the signs blended together. The crush behind the cordon was too great—too many signs being waved in the air. Sweat broke out over my back despite the relatively cool air.

What are we going to do if the guy isn't here?

"Cole? Anything?"

"Nothing. Let's keep going."

My worry escalated the farther right we went without seeing our driver, ratcheting upward to match my accelerating heartbeat.

Do I even have the phone number of the resort handy?

As we neared the end, a young man dressed in a crisp white shirt and sage-green slacks smiled kindly at me. Like most of the men in the crowd, he wore a traditional Balinese folded hat called an *udeng* on his head. His was white and the same green as his pants, intricately folded to form a peak at the front. "What resort are you looking for?" he asked me, his English accented but easily understandable.

My anticipation building at his words plummeted when I read the sign he held. *Haven* was written in a calming sage-green font, a stylistic lotus flower drawn beneath. I shook my head, my stomach tightening further. "Not yours, but thanks. We're looking for the driver from Pure Sands Resort."

A momentary cloud crossed the young man's face, then he quickly broke into a smile. "No problem! I will find him for you."

Before I could respond, the man disappeared into the crowd. Jetlag, coupled with culture shock, made me almost teary with gratitude at his simple kindness. I glanced at Cole, who shrugged. "I'm guessing he can probably do a better job than us. Let's wait here."

Less than a minute later, he returned, leading an older man with similar mahogany skin and black hair by the arm. The older man, who also wore a udeng on his head, held a piece of notebook paper with *Dawn Hammond* hand-scrawled on it. My shoulders sagged.

Oh, thank God!

"Here you go!" our savior cried. "I found him at the back." Then he stepped into the crowd, smiling at our profuse thanks before disappearing once more. I felt a slight pang at his exit.

Cole turned his attention to our driver. "You're taking us to Pure Sands Resort?"

"Yes," the man said, breaking into a creased smile. He wore a yellow smock and dark brown pants. "We go now. Come with!"

Beckoning, he pushed his way through the crowd toward the exit as we followed on the other side of the cordon. When Cole and I reached the end, he gave us a small bow, pressing his hands together in front of his chest. "Follow me."

We went through another set of glass doors into the

bright afternoon. Broiling sun and humid air, tinged with diesel fumes, assaulted my senses. A cacophony of cars, mopeds, and honking horns was all I could hear.

This was my peaceful Bali? The place of yoga, temples, and exotic adventures?

Trying to keep my disappointment in check, I followed our driver, with Cole just behind me. Our suitcases bumped over the rough cement as we pulled them behind us. The man led us into a parking garage and down several aisles before stopping at a dusty black sedan. I tried to ignore the dents and scratches.

He popped the trunk and grabbed my suitcase, hefting it inside, then added Cole's. Opening a rear door for me, he ushered me inside before getting behind the right-hand-drive wheel. Cole took a seat next to me. The car was stifling hot and smelled faintly of spicy food. At least it was clean, though the seats were stained.

"Ready?" the man beamed in the rearview mirror and passed us two bottles of tepid water. "Two and one-half hours to Pure Sands."

I relaxed a little when the car started, and air-conditioning blew from the vents. We pulled out of the parking garage, and I did my best to push down my uneasiness, more grateful than ever to have Cole by my side.

This is just the airport. They're always chaotic. Bali will only get better from here.

The driver pulled into a chaotic mass of traffic, much worse than the crowd at the airport. I braced both hands on my thighs as he missed hitting the bumper of a truck filled with cows. By an inch.

One mooed at me.

After merging onto the lane, the man glanced in his rearview mirror and smiled. "Welcome to Bali!"

Chapter Two

Cole

AS I WEDGED myself into the car's back seat for the long drive to our resort, I wondered if I'd be able to stay awake.

Not. A. Problem.

As soon as we left the airport and drove around a gigantic fountain featuring several monkey gods, sleepiness fled, and I started worrying about when the accident would happen. I'd been to Asia before, but only to big cities. There had been plenty of traffic in Beijing and Tokyo, but this was different. Cars, scooters—most with multiple people riding on them—bustled through any opening in the traffic, no matter how minute.

I glanced at Dawn, making sure she was okay. She looked back, her wide blue eyes clearly exhibiting her current emotion.

Wide-eyed fear.

I grabbed her hand and held it. It steadied me as much as her. But as we traveled through the dense madness of

Denpasar and then onto a slightly less-congested highway, a chaotic order to the traffic asserted itself. Drivers beeped their horns as they passed mopeds, letting the riders know to move to the shoulder. When traffic stopped at a light, the scooters weaved around the cars, massing at the front of the line.

Oncoming traffic passed our battered sedan within inches, yet no one collided with us. After an hour, it became clear that as long as everyone on the road knew the rules, the bedlam was actually predictable. The only accident we passed was a car on the side of the road, a tourist standing by the smoking hood and talking to a policeman. Our driver was relaxed and alert, further calming my nerves.

Message received. Don't drive here. Ever. Leave it to the experts.

Before we left San Bernadino, I'd asked Dawn about renting a car, but she said the resort would provide transportation.

Now I knew why.

As a large truck passed in the other direction, their mirror missing ours by a hair's breadth, Dawn made a strangled moaning sound. I turned to her and gave her a smile I hoped was reassuring, then murmured, "The traffic might make us a little uneasy, but there's a logic to it. We're still alive, so that's a good sign."

She pressed her lips tightly together and let go of my hand to tuck a lock of shoulder-length black hair behind her ear. A nervous smile crept across her face. "So far."

The two-lane, paved road wound and twisted along the coast, occasionally passing through towns. The traffic lessened but never thinned out completely. A bank of low, heavy clouds lay inland to our left, obscuring the interior of the island. Nearer to the road, we passed rice field after rice field. Some were flooded with water, while others were a vivid jade color.

After I became convinced we weren't going to die at any moment, I enjoyed the trip. We passed several ornate temples, and each town had a walled compound containing temples on a smaller scale. Arched streamers fluttered over the road, the breeze softly fluttering their black-and-white fabric. Others were yellow or red, and all were at least fifteen feet tall.

Our driver pointed to the left, toward the swirling, heavy clouds. "Mt. Agung!"

I wrinkled my forehead and looked at Dawn. "What did he say?"

"Mt. Agung," she replied, peering out the window. "It's a giant volcano, but I don't see a thing. I guess we'll have to take his word for it."

I nodded, filing the information away. She was the expert on Bali, not me. I was only along for moral support. Dawn and I had been friends since childhood. When I was eight, my family moved next door to hers. A tall, skinny kid, I didn't fit in. Though she was a year younger, Dawn took me under her wing. There wasn't much she could do about the bullies who made my life miserable, but her friendship made all the difference to a sad, lonely boy.

Until I finally grew into my body, and my tormentors realized I wasn't easy pickings anymore. But that didn't happen until high school. And Dawn stood by my side for all of it, even though she was popular and could have easily snubbed me.

Which was why I was protective as hell of her.

After announcing she planned to fulfill her dream of

traveling to Bali, I didn't even consider not accompanying her. Then she made the idea even more fun by suggesting we learn to scuba dive together. We could do our first official dives in Bali.

How could I pass that up? After all, water was my element.

We passed another road sign saying the town of Tulamben—and Pure Sands Resort—was ten kilometers closer. The place had an on-site dive center. From what I saw during my cursory research, most hotels and resorts did. Tulamben was a scuba destination, and a famous wreck, the Liberty, lay just offshore.

The road transitioned from easterly to northerly as we proceeded up the east coast of Bali. Now we were in rural confines, with stone walls enclosing brilliant green rice fields and orchards. The villages grew smaller, though each contained its walled temple complex. We passed a man walking an enormous pink-and-gray pig alongside the road. He carried a long stick and occasionally tapped the pig's side, keeping it to the shoulder of the pavement.

Dawn turned her head toward me, blinking slowly, and I answered with a grin.

Twenty kilometers later, we passed a boy riding a bicycle. Not that unusual, sure. Except his bike had no front wheel. He rode it along expertly, holding the front of the bicycle upright and balancing perfectly on his wheelie as he rode down the shoulder.

I couldn't help laughing. "We are definitely not in Kansas anymore."

Dawn shook her head, her face slack with wonder. "I thought I knew what to expect, but I didn't. It's so exotic!"

Another car passed with inches to spare, but I was used

to it by now. I relaxed further at Dawn's growing excitement. I was worried back there at the airport. When we hadn't been able to locate our driver, panic had marred her lovely face. I'd move heaven and hell to make sure this trip was everything she wanted. Dawn had gone through a divorce less than a year ago, and I hated seeing her so lost. Even if she was better off without Blake. Asshole Blake.

She deserved better than him anyway.

The town of Tulamben wasn't much to look at. Shops and restaurants lined each side of the main road, with several side roads leading toward the ocean to our right. We passed a sign for Haven, where the man who'd found our driver worked. The sign was painted a rich cream, and the sage-green name and lotus flower were prominently painted on it. A pond lay in front of the sign and an ornate plumeria arched overhead, pink-and-white blossoms drifting down to land in the pool.

Dawn's head craned around to inspect it as we passed.

A mile later, our driver turned right and slowly bumped along a rutted dirt road. Thick vegetation lined each side, creating a dim twilight even though it was early afternoon. A flash of movement caught my eye, and I pressed my face to the window. Several monkeys leaped between trees, then disappeared into the thick brush. We emerged back into the light and the driver stopped in front of a light-blue cinderblock building. The faded wooden sign outside read Pure Sands Resort. It wasn't much to look at, but I breathed a long sigh anyway.

Finally!

After days of air travel, over two hours in the car, and exhausting jet lag, we were here. Time to enjoy our vacation! We got out and the man unloaded our suitcases from the trunk. After another bow with pressed hands, he got back in his car and drove away.

"Well, I guess that's that," Dawn said and turned around.

We climbed a short flight of stairs and entered a plain, open-air lobby. Chipped white tile lined the floor and faded wooden carvings hung on the wall. A woman in an ornate flowered dress stood behind a long check-in counter, giving us the pressed hand salute in welcome.

Since this was Dawn's rodeo, I let her take the lead. She approached the scarred wooden counter and folded her arms on it, then nodded at the check-in clerk. "Hello. Dawn Hammond and Cole Foster. We have two rooms booked."

"Yes," the young woman said, smiling. "You are in adjoining rooms. Follow the path out of the lobby and your rooms are in the first block. Seven and eight. Here are your keys. Enjoy your stay." She handed us each a key with a blue plastic fob, but the numbers printed on the fob could hardly be made out.

"Who has which room?" Dawn asked.

"They are identical, so whichever you prefer."

"Okay." Dawn glanced at me. The dazed look was back, making my gut tighten. "Let's go, then."

We rose and pulled our suitcases behind us. I was slightly miffed the woman hadn't offered to have someone help Dawn with her luggage. "You want me to take your suitcase?"

She shot me a wan smile. "No, I'm fine. Let's get settled in, then meet in half an hour to explore. I guess it's up to us to find the restaurant and dive shop."

I frowned, not exactly thrilled with our reception, or the peeling paint on the buildings. We came upon a long row of one-story cinderblock rooms, painted a light yellow. The path continued toward the ocean, but Dawn stopped before room seven and handed me the other key. "I guess I'll take this one."

I gave her a smile, putting some confidence in it. "See you in half an hour."

As her door opened with a screech of rusty hinges, I continued to the next and ignored the tightness knotting my gut. My key turned easily, but the hinges made a similar noise to Dawn's door. I entered a stifling-hot white room. An air-conditioner sat in the lower half of a window but wasn't turned on.

I wrinkled my nose at the musty odor and quickly crossed the brown tile floor to turn on the air-conditioner. It whirred to life, though whirred wasn't the right word. More like clunked and lurched. Soon a steady stream of air emanated from the vents. I waved my hand in front of it. The air was cooler than the room, but barely.

"Hopefully it just needs to get going," I muttered, then examined the room. Dust had piled up on the floor in one corner. A king-sized bed with a sagging mattress and no headboard sat along one wall, and a plain wooden desk stood near the front door. I opened a door to find a small closet with a few plastic hangers. I rubbed the back of my neck, trying not to be disappointed.

It was a deal site, remember? You could hardly expect five-star accommodations for what we paid.

Entering the bathroom, the white tile looked clean, though it was chipped, and the grout was dark and ominous-looking. I crossed to the shower, then stumbled to a stop, gaping at the display of bare wiring next to the showerhead. A bark of laughter tumbled out of my mouth. "Pretty sure that's not up to code. That thing could kill me."

Shaking my head, my neck stopped when I glimpsed

the toilet. "What the *hell*?" I had heard about these when the swim team traveled to Beijing but had never actually seen an Asian toilet. A large porcelain basin lay flush with the floor, two ridges along the sides giving your feet traction as you stood.

Or squatted.

I was just thinking, *Did Dawn know about this?* when a firm rapping came from my front door.

When I opened it, Dawn stood there, shaking her head. "Cole. You know I'm not a diva. But this is not what I was expecting!" Then she stilled, hope filling her eyes. "Is your room better?"

"I doubt it, but come in and check it out. Maybe we can trade." Trying to disregard what the check-in woman said about the rooms being identical, I waved her in.

Dawn's face fell as she entered the still broiling-hot room. "It looks the same as mine. Is your bathroom... okay?"

My heart twisted as her eyes became glassy with what I was pretty sure were tears. "It has an Asian toilet. And the shower looks like an execution method."

"I had no idea! The website didn't show pictures of the bathrooms, so I just assumed they'd be standard ones!" She wrapped both arms around herself and started pacing. "I've been dreaming forever about cozy bungalows with courtyards and pools. I knew this place wasn't *that* fancy, but the rooms on their website looked clean and modern." She waved her arm around the shabby room, then pointed at the pile of dust in the corner. "Not like this. I can't stay here, Cole. I just can't!"

My heart thumped against my ribs. "I'm not sure we have a choice. Where else are we going to go?"

Dawn had opened her mouth to speak when a cockroach at least three inches long skittered across the tile floor in front of her feet. She screamed and bolted for the front door, opening it to run out. Groaning, I followed and tried to calm her down.

She gasped huge breaths, both hands pressed against her face. "That's it! We're out of here, Cole. We passed that Haven place on the way here. It's not far. Let's just go there instead."

"We don't know if they have any rooms!"

"Then we'll try somewhere else. I'm so sorry, Cole, but I can't stay here. I can't shower in that—" Another cockroach scurried across the threshold of the door, and she yelped, shuddering. Her face crumpled as she started crying, and that was all it took to melt my heart.

I pulled her against my chest and patted her back, warm and soft under my fingers. "We'll figure this out. I agree, suicide showers and two cockroaches in one minute is a bit much. Take it easy, Pooh-Bear."

She laughed weakly at her nickname and nodded against my chest. Shortly after we became friends as kids, I'd noticed Dawn was inseparable from a Winnie the Pooh backpack. It hadn't taken me long to christen her Pooh-Bear. She'd worn the backpack for several years, until it finally gave out and her mother had to throw it away. The nickname she gave me didn't appear for several more years and had more unsettled origins.

"We paid the balance before we left the US, and I'm not sure we can get a refund," I said.

"I'm sure we can't." She pulled away and wiped her face. "Cole, I've dreamed about this my whole life! Let's go check out Haven. Please!"

"Okay. Give me your key and I'll tell the lady in the lobby we changed our minds."

Picturing us bedding down in the jungle with the

monkeys, I retrieved our bags and headed up the path. I left Dawn to stand guard over our suitcases at the entrance to the access road. Holding both keys by their plastic handles, I shook them loosely as I climbed the stairs and entered the lobby.

Again.

Chapter Three

Dawn

AFTER COLE DISAPPEARED into the lobby, I glanced down the path toward our rooms. My breath was shaky and rapid. Was I overreacting? Making a huge mistake? Then I remembered the wiring in Cole's shower.

Nope. Not doing that.

Returning only minutes later, he waved off my apology, simply saying, "Okay, that's done. Let's go check out Haven." He darted his eyes all over my face before bending to take my suitcase. Then he turned to walk up the access road, dragging both bags. I stumbled after him.

He was right to worry. I was barely holding it together. My lifelong dream finally realized after picking myself up from the divorce.

Upon entering the room at Pure Sands, I'd tried to convince myself that air-conditioning wasn't necessary, and the stained bedspread wasn't *that* bad. To tell the truth, I'd been so shocked by the toilet and stained, dripping faucet, I hadn't even noticed the wiring in the shower. No doubt my bathroom had been the same as Cole's. Though I was not overly squeamish, the cockroaches had tipped me over the edge.

I need a distraction. I need to do something.

Cole dragged both suitcases by their handles, his triceps bulging from the effort. I frowned at his back, guilt eating me up. "Would you stop being all chivalrous? I can pull my own bag, you know."

He glanced over his shoulder and shot me a lopsided grin. "I know, but it's hot out here."

Quickening my steps, I grabbed the side of the handle, just below where Cole gripped it. I stopped, forcing him to do likewise. He turned to me with both brows raised.

"Thank you," I said firmly. "I've got this."

He stared at me for a long moment before nodding, then relinquished his hold on my suitcase. I moved around him, taking the lead. When we reached Tulamben's main road, I turned left. A nearly solid wall of vegetation spread out toward the ocean, and I marched straight down the left shoulder of the road—toward Haven. I bit my lip to contain the tears.

Please let it be a haven for me.

"Dawn..."

The concern in his voice made me walk even faster, emotion steadily building like a volcano inside me. I took a shuddering breath. "I'm fine, Cole."

"You're not fine, Dawn."

I was trotting down the shoulder of the road now. "Really, I am. This will work out."

Cole raised his voice to call out, "Hey, everyone knows you walk against traffic. You're on the wrong side of the road."

His words made me stop cold, and a laugh rushed from

my mouth even as tears overflowed. I had uttered the same exact two sentences to him years ago, after Cole had been bullied and made fun of. When I saw him after school, he had been hurrying home, nearly running with his shoulders hunched near his ears.

I followed him, the boy next door who was my closest friend. He was on the wrong side of the road, and I didn't want him to get hit by a car. So I called out those words to him. Cole stopped and faced me, an eleven-year-old boy with tears running down his face.

"They nicknamed me Scarecrow." His words dripped misery.

I closed the distance and stood before him. Even then, he was much taller. "Then wear it as a badge of honor. Turn their words around."

"What are you talking about? I'm tall and skinny. I'm clumsy. The nickname fits." He sniffled loudly.

"You're right. The nickname fits. Scarecrows are guardians of crops. They protect and defend what matters." The words poured out of my ten-year-old mouth of their own volition, possibly the most impactful ones I'd ever said. All I knew was he needed me at that moment. "Scarecrows *matter*, Cole. Wear your nickname with pride. For what it really means, not what some grade-school losers think it means."

His face still wet, he smiled faintly at me, the desire to believe lifting his expression. "Thanks for watching out for me."

I nodded at him. "You're my friend. That's what we do." I joined his side, and we began walking again, at a normal pace this time. "And you're welcome, Scarecrow." And with that, his private nickname was born.

Now, the sun beat down as I turned around to face him, a sob escaping from my chest. "I'm so sorry I got you involved in this."

Smiling, Cole stopped before me and wiped my cheeks with his thumbs. "You didn't get me into anything. We can do much better than that place. Let's keep going. On the other side of the road, okay?"

Nodding, I crossed over. I'd forgotten they drove on the left in Bali, but Cole hadn't. We continued past a restaurant and a clothing store. A car passed by, tapping its horn, and I gave a shaky laugh. Turning my head, I called out over my shoulder, "Thanks for watching out for me."

"You're my friend. That's what we do." He joined my side, wrapping one long arm over my shoulders as he pulled his suitcase with the other. I leaned into his solid presence—the one person who'd always been there.

The turnoff to Haven was farther than I thought. Anticipation built as the cream-colored sign grew larger. The lotus pond wrapped around on this side also, and the plumeria tree arched overhead. We crossed the asphalt and headed down the paved access road, once again back toward the ocean. The punishing temperature lessened as tall, leafy trees arched overhead, creating a remarkably serene and welcoming tunnel. As if the earth itself was wrapping its arms around us. It was quiet inside our cocoon. Cole scanned the trees several times, finally admitting he was looking for monkeys, but we didn't see or hear any. After a quarter mile, the light increased and sunlight slanted in, steam rising in the beams.

Cole peered down the lane. "The trees thin out ahead. I think we're almost there."

We continued and my smile lingered. I wasn't surprised

Cole was looking for animals. In grade school, we had bonded over being animal lovers and who had the better dog. Eventually, I reluctantly had to admit Cole's family did. Our family dog barked too much and chased after the mailman.

But my greatest love was children. I had been entranced at the age of four, when my little brother appeared. At twelve, I had a regular list of babysitting clients and was a nanny during high school. Becoming a teacher had been my natural choice for a career. From an early age, being part of a happy family with several kids was how I pictured my life.

And here I was—twenty-five, divorced, and childless.

And being a kindergarten teacher only seemed to make those facts more glaring.

Stop it! This is life. Period. And lots of people have it way worse.

My mind suitably chastened, I walked out of the tree tunnel. The road ended in a roundabout, and a towering pagoda fountain dominated the interior of the circle. Another lotus pond formed the basin of the fountain. We walked around the perimeter toward a cream-colored building with ornately carved wooden shutters. Matching doors were propped open.

We climbed a short flight of marble steps into a lobby. Green plants and more fountains were spaced around the room, and a stone panel carved with *Haven* amongst exotic flowers dominated the far wall. Three desks sat in front of the sign, with a woman behind the center one. Seeing us enter, she stood with a warm smile and bowed. Her black hair was up in a French twist, and she wore a white tunic and sage green skirt. She indicated two carved wooden chairs in front of her desk. "Welcome to Haven. Please have a seat."

Sweaty, dusty, and completely pitted-out after the walk, I gratefully plopped down, leaving my suitcase behind the chair. Cole took a seat next to me.

A second young woman appeared from nowhere, carrying a tray with two rolled towels and tumblers filled with fluid and ice. "Please, may I offer you a cool towel and lemongrass welcome drink?"

"That sounds amazing," Cole said with a smile. "Thank you."

I used the cool towel to wipe away the sweat and stress, inhaling its floral fragrance. The drink was lemon-ginger heaven.

This is it! This place is what I dreamed about.

We replaced our used towels on the tray and the woman disappeared again.

The first woman, whose nametag read Putra, seated herself behind her desk and woke the computer. "What is the last name on the reservation?"

My throat constricted mid-swallow and I nearly choked. Talk about being brought back to rude reality.

"We don't have a reservation," Cole said smoothly. "We're hoping you have a couple of open rooms for the next seven days?"

"Oh," Putra said, then quickly covered her surprise. "We are quite full at the moment, but let me see what is available."

I crossed my fingers as she tapped for several minutes. My heart knocked against my ribcage as I shot Cole a glance. He nodded reassuringly at me.

Putra broke into a broad smile. "You're in luck! We have one room left, and it's an ocean-view bungalow. Would that work?"

"We'll take it," I said at the exact same time Cole replied,

"How much is it?"

But Putra didn't miss a beat. "The bungalow is two million Rupiah per night."

I tried not to gasp at the enormous number. After two days of travel, the long car ride, and the trauma of cockroaches and Pure Sands, I wasn't capable of doing the conversion. So I nodded more confidently than I felt and said, "It sounds perfect. Thank you."

While Putra checked us in, I could see the wheels spinning in Cole's head as he tried to do the math, though he had to be as mentally fuzzy as me. My teacher salary didn't exactly provide a lavish budget. Cole's recent job position wasn't much better, but I swallowed down my misgivings.

The bill was a problem for future Dawn and Cole.

Putra stood and handed us a key with an ornately carved wooden fob. The Haven name with the logo was engraved on one side and *Damai* on the other.

"*Damai?*" I asked.

"It is the name of the bungalow," Putra said. "It means peace."

With that comforting news, a middle-aged man appeared and grasped the handles of our suitcases. "Please follow, and I will show you to your room."

We followed him down the stairs, then along a cement path stamped with imprints of leaves. Cole leaned over and whispered in my ear, "I already like this place *way* more."

"Me too. I just hope it doesn't bankrupt us." I couldn't voice my other fear out loud. That the bungalow we were being led to would prove as disappointing as the last room had been. What would we do then?

More plumeria trees were planted alongside the path,

and we walked through the scent of their pink, purple, and yellow flowers. Tall walls rose behind them. The path meandered, and at one point came to an intersection. The man continued straight ahead, and the sound of waves lapping onto the shore grew steadily louder.

Finally, he stopped before a solid, carved wooden door, with eight-foot plaster walls on each side. He took the key from me and opened the door. The sound of trickling water reached us immediately, and he indicated for us to enter.

I walked into a courtyard of at least forty square feet. Directly across was a fountain, the source of the trickling water. A miniature version of the massive pagoda in front of the lobby, this one also had a basin filled with lotus plants. An expansive gazebo with pillows on a daybed took up one corner. The far side was open to take advantage of the ocean view. The courtyard's floor consisted of neatly cropped grass with square stone pavers. They were set in precise rows leading to the floor-to-ceiling glass doors of a bungalow on our right.

Goose bumps rose on my arms as I took it all in. This was beyond my wildest dreams!

"Oh, wow," Cole breathed. "Look at that pool!"

I almost jumped at his words, pulled from my reverie. I was so entranced I hadn't even looked to our left. Next to the gazebo was a private rectangular pool, easily thirty feet long. Two loungers with sage-green cushions lay in the shallows, a step leading to the deeper section of the pool. Tall plaster walls enclosed the entire courtyard except for the front section of the gazebo facing the ocean, creating a private oasis.

The bellman stopped in the middle of the courtyard and let go of our suitcases. He walked to the wooden-framed windows opposite the pool and turned the key in the center one. Then he faced us. "Would you like me to show you the bungalow?"

Not wanting to appear any more stunned and idiotic than I already did, I shook my head. "No, we've got it. Thank you very much for bringing our luggage."

"My pleasure. The path outside leads to the ocean and continues to the restaurant. Feel free to enjoy the beach, and our dive center is also located at the entrance to the beach. Have a peaceful stay." After giving us the pressed-hands bow, the man left, closing the tall courtyard door behind him.

Cole and I slowly turned to each other. His mouth was hanging open, his eyes wide.

My expression had to be similar. "Are we going to have to take on second jobs to pay for this when we get home?"

He barked out a laugh, rubbing his face with both hands. His raspy jaw was audible as he scraped his palms over it. "I'm more than a little rummy, but if I did the math right, I think this place is less than one hundred and thirty dollars a night."

I reared back. "That can't be right!" Then I reconsidered. "Actually, it might be. Bali is known for having some spectacular low-priced accommodations, but they aren't advertised widely. I think our luck has changed!"

Haven was exactly the type of resort I'd watched on the endless Bali travel shows I'd eaten up for years. I couldn't wait to see all of it.

"Let's go check out the room." Cole opened the glass-paneled door and stepped inside, then moved so I could stand next to him.

The first thing I noticed was the blessedly cool air-conditioning. The large room smelled clean and a light, fresh scent permeated the room, tickling my nose as I inhaled deeply. The second thing I noticed was the bed.

As in one bed.

A king-sized bed with a gauzy, romantic mosquito net tied at its four corners faced the pool outside. A white comforter lay beneath a pile of sage-green and blue throw pillows.

At the same time, Cole and I turned our heads to stare at each other. In all the chaos, I hadn't thought about our sleeping situation.

"One bed, huh?" His face was carefully expressionless as he studied the room. It was generously sized, with a wall of wooden doors at the back, presumably the wardrobe. The half of the room not taken up by the bed contained a living area. Four solid chairs were placed around a wooden coffee table. Cole studied them and squared his shoulders. "I might be able to push two of those together and sleep there. You can have the bed."

The vision made me laugh. "How are you going to make that work? I couldn't sleep on two of those and I'm almost a foot shorter."

"I'll pile some blankets on the floor, then."

"Cole, stop it. We're both adults. We can sleep in the same bed."

He looked dubious, but he clearly wasn't enthusiastic about sleeping on the marble floor. "You sure?"

I propped a hand on my hip. "Girls sleep together in one bed all the time. It's no big deal."

"I'm not a girl, Dawn."

"You're also not my boyfriend." I cocked my head. "I'm pretty sure I can manage to keep from assaulting your virtue, Scarecrow."

At least I'm pretty sure I can.

There was no denying Cole had grown from an ugly duckling into a rather spectacular swan.

He broke into that crooked smile I loved. "Pretty sure I can too. Okay, I promise to keep my hands to myself if you do the same."

I held up my right hand, middle fingers pressed together with my thumb folded over my bent pinky, and grinned. "Scout's honor."

Chapter Four

Cole

"WOULD you hurry up in there? I'm about to fall asleep on my feet!" I called to the closed bathroom door.

"I'm almost done. This bathroom is amazing!"

I couldn't argue with that. The whole bungalow—and its courtyard area—was astonishing. Who would have thought I'd ever be grateful to cockroaches? Crossing to the mirror over the desk, I finger combed my light-brown hair, making sure it was neat. My button-down shirt and cargo shorts were wrinkled but wearable. I'd showered first in the massive outdoor shower, a circular rain showerhead washing over me as I watched the clouds overhead. The tall surrounding walls provided plenty of privacy.

But while waiting for Dawn to get cleaned up, exhaustion hit me like a train barreling down the tracks. I was familiar enough with jet lag to recognize the symptoms. We needed to eat dinner soon. Before I fell asleep in my soup.

The bathroom door opened, and Dawn swept out. She was dressed in a light-blue sundress, and her black hair was pulled into a silver barrette. I tried not to stare, but she'd always been able to floor me simply by existing. Her blue eyes sparkled as she slipped into sandals. "Let's go check out the restaurant. An hour ago, I wasn't hungry at all. But now I'm starving."

I pulled on a pair of sports sandals. "Yeah, I'm the same way. Jet lag, I guess." I crossed the room to open the door.

"Well, look at you," she drawled. "Fancy shirt and nice shorts. You'll have girls coming at you from all angles. Good thing I'm here to protect you."

I laughed and shook my head. "Just trying to keep up with you."

The sky was fully dark now, and ornate metal lamp-posts lit our way as we walked down the concrete path to the beach. The path continued parallel to it, toward the restaurant and resort pool. The ocean softly lapped against the shore, drawing my eye to a hut as we passed by.

After unpacking earlier, we'd wandered around the resort and were pleased to find the dive shop so convenient to our bungalow. We went in to ask if we could join the dive trip the following morning.

The man inside nodded. He wore a staff Haven rash guard and board shorts. His black hair was cut short, and I guessed he was in his thirties. "Of course. We have only one other couple diving. The resort is at capacity, but most guests are here for a yoga retreat."

I glanced at his nametag and said, "Thanks, Wayan. Sounds perfect. We're brand-new divers and need to rent everything."

"No problem. I'll take good care of you—don't worry."

. . .

Now, the lights of the open-air restaurant called. I took a closer look at the resort pool as we passed. It was at least twenty yards long with a solid deep end.

Might be able to get some workouts in while I'm here.

I swept my gaze across the ocean, imagining what might lie beneath. "You looking forward to our first official dive tomorrow?"

Dawn hesitated a moment before answering. "I am, but I'm a little nervous."

Two months ago, when we'd booked our trip here, she'd further surprised me by wanting to learn to scuba dive. She didn't have to twist my arm—I loved anything to do with the water. She explained it was a way to step into the unknown —her after-Blake world. So we'd signed up for open water certification at a local dive shop in San Bernadino and received our certification cards two weeks ago.

Even I had to admit learning to scuba dive had a serious learning curve. And Dawn had done great in the class. "It'll be a piece of cake," I said.

"I assumed we'd be going out on a boat. But at least I don't need to worry about getting seasick if we enter from the beach. And the wreck sounds exciting."

Wayan had explained that Tulamben's main diving attraction was a ship that had been sunk during World War II and lay a short distance offshore. The entry was from a clearing a short distance away. The Liberty was covered with coral growth and safe even for beginners.

"Sounds like an amazing first dive for us," I said as we approached the restaurant. "I'm glad there's only one other couple diving."

"Yeah, me too—less pressure that way, since we're beginners. I wanted to challenge myself, and here we are."

"Exactly."

The restaurant lay beneath an enormous thatched roof. Support pillars made from the trunks of palm trees were placed evenly throughout and the tables were well-spaced for privacy.

A woman walking by with a pitcher of water smiled at them. "Feel free to take any table you like."

We chose a table for two that overlooked the pool, with the beach just beyond. The young woman who'd been carrying the water approached our table to fill our glasses. She wore what I was discovering was the typical Balinese dress of a long skirt paired with a colorful tunic. "Welcome. I am Kirana. What would you like to drink?"

"Beer," I said. "What do you have that's local?"

"Bintang. Large and small bottles."

"Large for me," I said.

"I'll take a small," Dawn said to her.

My jaw dropped when Kirana brought our beers. Dawn's was the standard twelve ouncer, but mine was huge, nearly twice the size. I grinned as we clinked bottles. "Here's to sleeping well tonight."

"I don't think that will be a problem," Dawn said.

Easy for you to say.

When I had glimpsed that king-sized bed, I didn't know whether it represented my biggest dream or nightmare. Although Dawn and I had always been strictly friends, and I had faithfully attended her wedding, I was still a red-blooded man. And I had eyes. My sweet next-door neighbor had grown into a gorgeous woman, and I wasn't any more immune to that than any other man.

Maybe it was a good thing she'd always see me as the skinny, awkward kid she'd nicknamed Scarecrow. I'd never stand a chance with her anyway.

But sleeping in the same bed with her every night for the next week? That was going to involve some serious discipline on my part. Good thing I was a pretty determined guy.

Half an hour later, we were both feeling the effects of the beer more than normal. I pointed at her dinner and gave her a mock scowl. "You finally make it to Bali, and you're having a club sandwich?"

She shrugged, unrepentant. "I'm easing into it. Unlike you, I don't have a cast-iron stomach."

I scraped my last piece of chicken from its wooden stick, the spicy peanut sauce tickling my taste buds all the way down. "Suit yourself. The sate is fantastic and not too spicy."

"Maybe tomorrow, then."

Kirana returned and collected our empty plates. "Is your bungalow satisfactory?"

Dawn laughed and sat back in her chair. "Beyond satisfactory. We're in *Damai*."

The server inclined her head and smiled. "That one has a beautiful view. Very romantic." She balanced our plates on her forearm. "If you are interested, we offer an exotic dinner for a different taste of Bali. Please let us know by noon if you would like to order it, as some of the dishes take time to prepare."

Dawn narrowed her eyes. "How exotic?"

The woman burst into a broad smile. "The meal consists of several courses that we Balinese eat regularly. But they tend to be... unusual to visitors."

That made my ears perk up. I loved exotic food. "What kind of dishes?"

"We serve red lawar, which contains blood."

I grinned as Dawn slumped in her seat.

The server continued. "And also sago worms, which are a type of... grub?... I think is the correct term in English."

It sounded fabulous to me, but Dawn was slightly green. She shook her head. "Thanks, but no, thanks. That's a little too exotic for me."

After I signed the room charge slip, I shot Dawn a grin. "Come on! Live a little."

"I do want to live. That's why I'm not drinking blood and eating slugs."

"I don't think it's pure blood. More like that is one of the ingredients."

"No, Cole." But she was smiling, so I had hope.

We pushed to our feet and headed back to our room. She glanced up at me. "You don't sleep in the nude or anything, do you?"

I generally slept in my underwear, but there was no way that was happening with her around. "No. I brought a pair of pajama bottoms. You want me to wear a T-shirt?"

She laughed softly. "Not on my account. I've seen your chest, Cole. Nothing new there."

"Ouch. I work hard with those weights, I'll have you know."

"Oh, I'm not denying that. Only letting you know the sight of your bare torso isn't likely to make me faint dead away."

"What about your bare torso?" The words escaped my mouth before I even realized they had been formed, so I covered it with a big grin.

She arched a brow and matched my smile. "I brought along a tank top and terrycloth sleep shorts. Just stay on your side, buster."

"What about you? I don't want to have to defend myself in the middle of the night."

She yawned hugely. "I don't think that's going to be a problem. I'll probably fall asleep before I crawl into bed."

"Yeah, me too." That was one benefit of the massive jet lag. And the large Bintang. I wouldn't have to lie awake thinking about how I was finally in bed with Dawn, yet nothing had changed between us.

Then again, I wasn't sure I wanted that.

Wasn't I?

Chapter Five

Dawn

WHEN COLE and I entered the bungalow after dinner, housekeeping had performed a turn-down service. The nightstand lamps were turned on a low setting, providing a romantic glow through the mosquito net now fully draped over the bed and nightstands. I hadn't noticed any mosquitos around the resort, so I was sure the net was for ambience, not protection. Chocolates lay on our pillows with a plumeria flower.

Cole and I turned to each other with slightly awkward smiles, but I was too damn tired to joke about wasted romantic gestures. After brushing my teeth, I changed into my tank top and shorts, wondering if I should wear a bra to bed.

But why? It's Cole—he's not interested in me that way.
Especially now.

I crawled into bed and turned off my bedside lamp as Cole entered the bathroom. I knew him well enough to understand he wasn't accompanying me on this trip out of pity. He genuinely cared about me and was excited about being somewhere as exotic as Bali. But he'd always seen me as a friend, nothing more. And men weren't on my agenda anyway. I couldn't deny I was still smarting from the divorce—and the fact that Blake blamed me for our failure to have a family.

Yeah, but it wasn't like he'd been interested in solving any problems we might have had.

I blew out a long exhale that wasn't quite a snort. *Enough! No more thinking about that.*

I was easily distracted from those futile thoughts when Cole exited the bathroom, strolling across the room in his blue plaid pajama bottoms.

And no shirt.

I mostly kept my eyes averted but couldn't resist a few peeks. Despite my teasing about his chest and abs, Cole was very hard to ignore. He climbed through the opening on the net on his side of the bed and turned off his lamp, plunging the room into darkness.

"Night, Pooh Bear," he said and yawned loudly.

I smiled. "Sweet dreams, Scarecrow." Then I closed my eyes.

AND THAT WAS ALL I knew until 3:00 a.m., when I awoke completely alert and unable to fall back asleep. I tried to lie still so I didn't disturb Cole, who slept on the other side of the bed. Despite counting sheep, pretending I lay on a cloud, and other sleep-inducing measures, I was wide awake. Finally, I glanced at my watch, and now it was after five.

Even with the drapes closed, the room wasn't completely dark. Pale moonlight provided plenty of illumination as I turned my head to watch Cole. Breathing deeply, he slept on his back with one arm bent above his head. The covers were pulled down to his waist.

Watching him unobserved was a rare luxury, and I took advantage. His sculpted pecs were nearly smooth, with only a light amount of chest hair. The soft light emphasized the multiple ridges of his abdomen. He was a work of art, stunning in the moonlight.

So why am I torturing myself by watching him? He might not pity me, but he's never seen me as anything but a friend. And I need my friend more than ever.

Tossing back the covers, I quietly slid out of the bed and padded across the room. A small coffee station sat on the desk, with a kettle and a selection of instant coffees. My research on Bali had already informed me the island's inhabitants loved instant coffee, especially sweetened coffee. I lifted the kettle off its platform and tiptoed into the bathroom to fill it. After returning, I placed it on the warmer and turned it on.

I shot a guilty glance at the bed, not wanting to wake Cole. But without light, I couldn't identify the coffee packets lined up in the small tray. Retrieving my cell phone, I turned on the flashlight, tilting it this way and that. The water hissed as it warmed up.

A rustling came from the bed and Cole's lamp turned on. He appeared at the foot of the bed and stretched both arms overhead with a loud groan. I tried not to stare.

"Man, I slept like the dead." He crossed to the closet lining the back of the bungalow and pulled a dark orange T-shirt out of the closet. As he crossed the room, he pulled it on. *Texas Longhorns Swimming* was screen-printed across the front. "How about you?"

I turned on the desk lamp since there was no need to be

stealthy anymore and picked out a packet with coffee, creamer, and sugar all in one. "I woke up at three and couldn't get back to sleep. Sorry if I woke you. I tried to be quiet."

"It's fine. I'm wide awake."

I poured the powder into a mug and added the hot water. "There's some decaf here. You want one?"

Cole dug through the tray of packets. "No way. I want caffeine this morning." He picked out a different three-in-one variety and I poured water in his cup.

"Let's go outside and watch the sunrise," I said and drew open the drapes covering the front of the bungalow. It was lighter out now, and the top of the courtyard wall was slightly visible against the sky. The early morning air was warm and smelled faintly of incense. I inhaled deeply and smiled as I stepped outside.

Cole pointed with his chin at the roofed pavilion in the corner. "The gazebo faces the ocean. Let's sit in that."

Nodding, I strolled across the stone pavers, cool under my feet. A row of them led between the base of the pool and the gazebo. Balancing my coffee carefully, I climbed onto the king-sized daybed that filled the entire structure, edging to the far side to make room for Cole. Pillows were piled up at the head of the bed, giving a wide-open view of the beach and ocean beyond. An orange stripe on the horizon signaled dawn's approach before us, fading to indigo, then black as stars glimmered to the west.

I clinked my mug to his. "To our first morning in Bali."

"I'll drink to that," he said and then did just that.

"So have you given up decaf now that you're an old, retired guy?" I asked, my eyes drawn to the tattoo faintly visible on the inside of his bicep as he lifted his cup.

He smiled, his teeth flashing in the dim light. "Yeah.

Caffeine is a legal substance, but you could get disqualified and fined if you had too much in your system. Seemed like a dumb risk to take, so I went with decaf. It seemed to wake me up most of the time."

"Or maybe the ten miles of swimming every day did that."

He laughed softly. "Not that much, but I don't miss those grueling days."

As long as we'd known each other, I had just learned something new about him. "I didn't think you even drank regular coffee."

He turned those hazel eyes to me, a humorous glint in them. "We haven't woken up together too many times, Dawn."

I laughed. "Touché. And it only seems fitting—decaf is too tame for the guy who wants to drink blood and eat bugs."

"Exactly. I don't mind taking risks, but not unnecessary ones. And I'm not giving up on the exotic meal, either."

I repressed a shudder. "I have an acceptable compromise. You order the bugs and I'll eat a club sandwich. At the next table."

He laughed. "Coward."

The entire eastern sky was awash in color now, orangish-yellow at the ocean's edge, changing to pink, then purple before becoming a deep blue I'd never seen before. "One step at a time. Just being here is a big step."

"I know. I'm proud of you."

Cole put down his empty cup and drew me against him. I settled against his shoulder, grateful for the contact. Grateful for what he offered me. Together, we watched a new day dawn.

"This will work," I said before reaching behind myself to unzip the wetsuit using its attached leash. I pulled it off and folded it over my arm. Next to me, Cole stood in a rash guard and swim trunks, correctly surmising the small dive shop would have difficulty finding a wetsuit for his large frame. Fortunately, the ocean was warm enough he didn't need the insulation.

Our divemaster Wayan rubbed his hands together. "That's everything. Let's go outside. Your kits are all assembled."

We exited the cool dive shop and stopped before a picnic table. Five scuba kits stood on top. Each consisted of a silver tank with its vest-like buoyancy compensation device attached. A regulator was fastened at the top of the tank, one hose leading to the BCD to provide inflation. Another couple near our age stood next to the table, chatting. The woman's long brown hair was coiled into a bun at the nape of her neck. The man was only a couple of inches shorter than Cole and even more muscular. His nearly black hair coupled with pale blue eyes were a striking combination.

Wayan stopped next to them and turned to Cole and me. "This is the other couple in our group. Cole and Dawn, meet Quinn and Steph." All four of us shook hands, and the couple greeted us with warm smiles.

That put me slightly at ease. "We should probably warn you," I said. "We're brand-new divers. This will be our first official dive after certification."

"Congrats," Quinn said with a smile. "You picked a great place to start. We've been here for over a week and have dived the Liberty a bunch of times. We can't get enough of it."

"Quinn and Steph are quite experienced and familiar with the two sites we'll be diving today," Wayan added. "So they might dive apart from us."

Cole grinned. "I take it that's a polite way of saying you're going to stay away from us train wrecks?"

"Not at all!" Steph said with a laugh. Both she and Quinn spoke with American accents. "I'm not too far ahead of you. We'll all have a great time."

Wayan pointed to two weight pouches, which slid into a pocket of the BCD to allow the diver to sink from the surface. But now they lay on the table in front of each tank. "We will carry our own weight pouches and wetsuits down the beach. Our tanks will be brought to the dive site separately, so we prefer for the kits to be as light as possible. It's a bit of a walk to the entry point." He grabbed his two pouches filled with lead weights, folded his wetsuit over an arm, and led the way toward the beach.

Picturing someone hefting our heavy tanks into a pickup truck for the journey, I was more than happy to carry my pouches. Cole and I fell in behind the other couple as we descended a short flight of stone steps and onto the sand.

The black sand.

That had been a bit of a shock when we had explored the resort the previous afternoon. I knew Bali had black sand beaches but didn't realize one was located in Tulamben. The sand was powdery soft and a very dark gray. I could easily imagine its volcanic origins.

As we passed by, a worker was placing a line of loungers on Haven's beach. The ocean was a beautiful turquoise and gently lapped upon the shore. I turned my head to survey the interior of the island and stumbled to a dead stop.

"Oh my God! Cole, check this out."

The previous day's heavy cloudbank was gone, and now the interior of the island was crystal clear. An enormous brown-and-green volcano reached toward the sky, dwarfing everything around it. The massive cone looked close enough to touch.

Wayan realized we'd stopped and pointed at it. "Mt. Agung."

"Our driver pointed to it yesterday, but it was covered in clouds," Cole said in a low, awed voice.

"It looks like it's right on the other side of the highway," I said.

"No," Wayan said with a smile. "Farther than that. It looks close because it's so big. It last erupted several years ago, and Tulamben was evacuated for months."

"I can see why." I resumed my stroll with Cole at my side. Quinn and Steph walked in front of us. Curiously, the volcano further put me at ease, a reminder of the Bali I had dreamed of and seen videos of. Yet another sign Haven was the right place for us.

Several resorts lined the beach, which I remembered from our passage on the road yesterday. Looking back, it was hard to believe how traumatized and devastated I'd been. Haven had been exactly that for us. The beach thinned out and we hopped onto a sea wall, continuing single file. Carrying the weight pouches and wetsuit made it somewhat of a balancing act and I wobbled a bit.

"Want me to carry anything?" Cole asked from behind.

"No, I'm fine. Just a little off balance." I'd been a volley-ball player in high school, not a gymnast. But if someone was bringing our tanks around by the road, this was the least I could do.

Fortunately, the beach expanded once again, and soon the wall ended. I increased my pace to join Steph's side. "So, you two have been here for a while?"

"Yeah. We're staying two weeks, and today is day ten, I think." Then she turned to Quinn. "Is that right?"

He grinned. "Hell if I know. You're in charge of the schedule. I handle the diving."

"It's amazing how fast the time goes," Steph said.

"What made you choose Bali?" Cole asked as he joined my other side.

"We're friends with the yoga instructor here," Quinn said. "And neither of us could think of a better place to spend our honeymoon."

"Your honeymoon!" I said. "Congratulations."

"Thanks," Steph replied, shooting a long look at Quinn. He returned it with interest, and I couldn't help smiling.

The resort we were passing ended, and we emerged into a large clearing. Short grass covered the area with coconut palms soaring overhead. Picnic tables were spaced around the clearing and several groups were in the process of putting on or taking off scuba equipment.

Wayan stopped at the nearest empty table and pointed at the calm blue ocean. "The wreck is less than one hundred feet offshore. We'll kit up and it's an easy entry off the beach." He moved off to talk to several other divemasters standing in a circle.

I didn't see a road. Sweeping my gaze around the area, confusion set in. "Our tanks aren't here yet?"

Quinn grinned as he leaned back against the table. His eyes held a speculative gleam, like he was looking forward to something. "No, they'll be along in a minute. Steph and I are old hands at this process."

"Here they come now," Steph added, pointing at the beach. Then she turned to watch us.

I followed where she indicated, and my jaw dropped. Cole's expression was similar.

Quinn and Steph both laughed at our reaction.

A line of five women walked toward us up the beach, following the same path we had taken. Each balanced an assembled scuba kit on her head. Two used a hand to steady the heavy burden, while the other three walked with the tank completely balanced, their arms moving freely at their sides. A tiny older woman led the procession.

"What?" Cole asked, drawing his brows downward. "I thought they'd bring our stuff by cart or a vehicle of some sort."

"Me too," I murmured.

He straightened. "I'm going to go take mine from her."

Steph laughed again. "Don't do that. Wayan explained it to us already. They're tank porters and this is how they make their living. Wayan's wife and mother are in that line. His mother is the tiny one—she was one of the first porters in Tulamben."

Cole didn't look convinced. "I feel terrible. Those tanks probably weigh almost as much as they do."

"Good thing women are strong, huh?" I added, and Steph laughed.

Wayan had made his way back over. "They're very strong. This has been our way of life for generations. They take pride in their job and do it well. My mother, Melati, is in the lead, and Diah, my wife, is behind her."

Quinn approached and clapped Cole on the shoulder. "I had misgivings about it too. Think of it as one of the exotic customs you discover when you travel. That helps. A little, anyway."

Cole's eyes didn't leave the wizened woman who carried his tank, and my heart warmed at his obvious concern. Melati wore a tunic and a long colorful skirt, but the others were dressed in pants and T-shirts. As she approached the table, Melati deftly tipped her head forward, placing the kit on top with a solid thunk. Wayan spoke to them in rapid Indonesian, and the women smiled at us and gave us the Bali pressed-hands greeting bow. I returned it, feeling slightly self-conscious. The woman who carried my tank nodded, her smile growing wider, and I turned to her.

"Thank you," I said. "Do you speak English?"

"Some," she said. "I am Diah. Wayan is my husband." She stood with a fluid grace I could never match.

Must come from balancing fifty pounds on your head. "Pleased to meet you, Diah. How do you say thank you in Indonesian?"

She inclined her head. "*Terima kasi.*"

I repeated the phrase back to her and she replied, "*Sama sama.*"

The women headed back down the beach, clustered together and chatting as they walked. Wayan turned to us and clapped his hands. "Let's get ready to dive!"

Chapter Six

Cole

AS DAWN and I walked toward the shore, I placed a hand on the back of her tank to steady her. The extra weight wasn't a challenge for me to carry, but it was a different story for her. Wayan was to Dawn's left with Quinn and Steph on his other side. The water was calm, hardly making a splash as it swept upon the black sand.

I stepped into warm water, and some of the tension I'd been carrying dissolved now that I was entering my natural element. As we waded in, I continued steadying Dawn.

She smiled when she noticed it. "Got my back, huh?"

"Always."

When we were thigh-deep, we slipped on our dive fins. Wayan scanned the group. "Any questions?"

Four heads shook back at him, so he put the regulator in his mouth and gave us the thumbs-down to descend. My BCD made a hissing noise, air escaping, as I depressed the deflator valve. After a glance to confirm Dawn was doing likewise, I tipped forward and began finning. Immediately, I sank below the surface. The sea floor was rippled black sand. I touched my fingers to the soft ground, realizing I was about to hit the bottom, and added air to my BCD until I floated just above the surface.

Wayan took the lead, and we fanned out behind him, the two couples slightly separated. I cleared my ears several times as the depth increased, and glanced at the dive computer on my wrist. We were twenty-five feet below the surface and the sandy bottom continued at the same gentle slope. We stopped at a purple anemone, its tentacles waving back and forth in the gentle surge. Movement caught my eye and I gasped. Surprised delight filled me as three clown-fish fluttered through the ivory-colored tentacles.

Wayan beckoned to Dawn and me, and we carefully moved closer, taking care not to touch the poisonous anemone. Nemo in the flesh! The fishes' colors were nearly fluorescent—vivid orange with irregular white-and-black bars between. I met Dawn's eyes, which had to be as excited and huge as mine must be.

As we continued, more isolated coral heads appeared. Wayan mostly ignored them, but I swam nearer to one as we passed, unable to ignore the riot of color. Tiny fish covered every surface, dropping into the colorful coral for protection as I neared.

Dawn had stopped to wait for me, and I hurried to catch up. We rejoined the group, and I glanced at more coral heads as we passed by, ambivalent about passing up such amazing life to see a shipwreck.

Oh well, we have to come back this way. I'll get closer on the way back.

As our depth increased, I had to add air to my BCD to keep from dropping onto the sandy bottom. But I couldn't figure out how much—too much and I'd shoot up ten feet and have to dump it. The tank wanted to shift from side to side, making me clumsy. My eyes shifted to Dawn, but she finned effortlessly, perfectly horizontal in the water.

Huh. She's better at this than me.

Another glance at my computer informed me we were now over fifty feet down. I looked up and the soft peaks of waves were easily visible on the surface. Wayan performed a slight course correction and led us left. I studied the blue in the distance, able to discern a vague darker area but unable to differentiate it. As we swam on, Quinn and Steph diverged, though still remained within sight. Wayan held our depth steady, which caused the dark bottom to drop farther and farther below.

In the distance, it materialized out of the hazy blue water.

An enormous steel structure stretched out lengthwise before me. Awe prickled down my spine at the sheer size of the ship—over three hundred feet long. We angled up, finning up the hull and toward the deck. Several massive schools of fish circled the wreck, balling up for safety as swift predators darted in from all sides. We reached the deck, and an explosion of coral grew on every exposed surface. A huge barracuda hung motionless in the water, mere feet away. We came upon a thick cloud of blue-striped snappers, and they gently parted as I approached, forming a solid wall of fish all around me. I swam out of the cloud and turned my head to see Dawn doing the same. She reached out to take my hand.

I squeezed back, grateful to share this wondrous experience with her. Wayan led us around the superstructure, passing a flight of stairs now encrusted with coral.

We continued along the steel deck, but despite being in a weightless environment, I felt cumbersome and awkward.

I pressed a finger to a bare section of the deck below me to keep from bumping into it and couldn't get the hang of adding air to become neutral in the water.

Fumbling with the inflator valve, I finally located the correct button and gave it a long burst of air. That unbalanced me, so I waved my free arm to right myself again. I winced at the realization I'd added too much air to my BCD. The extra air caused me to rise upward, and a rapid ascent was one of the most dangerous things a diver could do.

Oh shit. I am a hot mess here.

I grabbed for the inflator hose again, fumbling once more. The more I hurried, the worse it got. I dropped the damn thing, then had to pick it up again. Meanwhile, I had risen at least ten feet and was still climbing.

Then another hand appeared on my inflator, pressing the deflator button. I glanced over to see the hand was attached to Quinn. He held down the button a short while, his movements sure and confident, and I stopped ascending and became neutral once again.

He gave me an okay signal, both brows raised.

Slightly embarrassed, I nodded back.

He patted my shoulder twice and swam off to rejoin Steph. Wayan and Dawn had turned around, both watching carefully. With heat warming my face, I gave them both an okay signal and continued the dive. Dawn was moving through the water with ease, and as the dive progressed, I found myself watching her as much as our incredible surroundings.

She'd wanted to learn scuba to challenge herself. Her divorce had shaken her confidence. Hell, it had shaken her identity. She'd been nervous during the class, and I had supported her the whole way, assuring her she could do it.

And look at her now. She's better at this than I am.

When we were younger, both of us had been full of dreams, our image of what the future would bring. But only I realized my greatest goal. Dawn's might not have been as sweeping as mine, but it was no less important. She had ended up heartbroken.

But she refused to stay there.

Wayan stopped to show Dawn a colorful sea slug—a nudibranch. After looking, she waved me over, moving away so I could see it. The four-inch creature was covered in a sweeping pattern of black, red, and green, with a fantastic rosette on its back.

I glanced at Dawn and winked. *Yeah, I admit it's pretty. But nothing down here compares to you.*

I was comfortable only thinking that last sentence, not saying it out loud. That was how it had always been. I'd loved Dawn from afar for most of my life. Sharing a bed wasn't going to change that.

Right?

Watching her sent my mind in directions I didn't want, so I turned my head to study the first thing that caught my eye. Which happened to be Quinn. He swam up to Steph, then fluttered his fins to stop as he took her hand. His movements were effortless and confident.

That guy knows what he's doing. A lot more than I do, at least for now.

I was too comfortable in the water to put up with my rookie ineptitude as a diver. For the rest of the dive, I made a point to study both Wayan and Quinn, mimicking their position in the water. As we headed back to the shore, I got better at detecting when I became too buoyant and let air out of my BCD, pleased with my progress.

After we exited the water, we set our kits back on the

picnic table for the women porters to bring back to Haven. I still wasn't comfortable with the procedure, though I wasn't about to deprive anyone of their livelihood.

The four of us made our way down the beach, and I caught up to Quinn. "Thanks for your help down there."

"No problem. There's so much to figure out at first, and I could see what the problem was. Easy-peasy."

"I'm guessing you've been diving a while."

Steph leaned forward and looked over Quinn's chest at me. "He's a dive instructor."

I broke into laughter. "That explains it. Don't feel you need to be shy about correcting me. I felt like a lumbering bear."

"You were fine," Quinn said quietly. "Just keep at it and you'll get the hang of it in no time. You guys diving tomorrow?"

"No," Dawn said. "The following day we are, but we're planning on exploring tomorrow. Any recommendations?"

"Ubud is fantastic!" Steph said. "The front desk can arrange a car and driver to show you around."

Dawn nodded. "I've heard about it. We'll check it out."

I kept from smirking, having a feeling there wasn't much about this island Dawn didn't know.

LATER THAT AFTERNOON, we spent some time in our private pool. Dawn was lazing in the water while I lay on one of two loungers sitting in the shallow end. "What time do we leave for our tour tomorrow?"

"Ten. Our driver will be waiting outside the lobby. They arranged quite the excursion. Rice terraces, the city center of Ubud, and plenty of time to explore by ourselves."

"Sounds fun."

After diving, Dawn had arranged for the tour in the lobby while I took a shower in our fabulous outdoor bathroom. Now, an easy lassitude washed over me—I was very close to falling asleep. I turned over and slipped into the water, joining Dawn in the main section of the pool, which was four feet deep all the way across. "I gotta stay awake. The trick to adjusting is to avoid naps and power through until evening."

"I hope I can sleep past three."

"That would be a plus. So, what did you think of your first dives?"

Dawn leaned against the tiled wall of the pool. She wore a light-blue bikini and I made sure to keep my eyes on her face, which was no easy task. But it was easier when her face exploded into a beautiful smile that lit her from within. "That was incredible! So many fish, and the sea fans... I don't even have words for the experience."

"Yeah, I hardly knew what to focus on."

"Did you see that incredible fish on the second dive?" Dawn asked. After diving the Liberty, our second dive had been on a wall in front of the resort.

I crouched in the water, submerging up to my neck. "Which one? They were all incredible."

"I can hardly describe it. It was black and orange on top, with huge white spots on the bottom and big orange lips."

I grinned. "Sounds more like a clown than a fish. Point it out if you see it again."

"Don't worry. I will."

I sighed wistfully. "You sure are a natural."

Her smile turned mischievous. "Do I detect a little jealousy in that tone?"

"Not in the slightest. I was pretending to be a lumbering idiot so you would look better."

Her smile fell, and she cocked her head.

I briefly closed my eyes. "I'm kidding, Dawn! You dove circles around me. But you'd best look out, missy, because I was much better after the second dive."

Her smile returned, making me feel better. "I've never been better than you at something involving water before. I want to enjoy the experience. At least until you get your wiggles worked out and mop up the floor with me."

Joining her side, I slid my feet along the bottom of the pool so the water covered me to mid-chest. "Pretty sure we're on an equal playing field this time. Don't think I have the advantage."

She raised a brow. "Hardly. Not when it involves water."

I nudged her with my shoulder. "I only discovered that because of you."

When I was nine years old and we had started summer break, Dawn asked if I wanted to take swimming lessons with her. Both of us knew how to swim, but it was more splashing around. She was interested in taking serious lessons, all summer long. I was less enthusiastic, imagining yet another way for my peers to torment me. But I could never say no to Dawn, not even then. So I'd stood by her side as we entered the pool that June morning. She was full of excitement, and I was full of trepidation.

Even though I was a year older, the coach took one look at my weedy, clumsy form and put me in the same class as Dawn. First thing, the coach had us swim to the end of the twenty-five-yard pool to gauge our ability. I still remember how distant the far end looked to me. My heart pounded as Dawn and I waited for our turn, with me picturing not being able to make it even halfway down—plenty of kids weren't able to. Then we were in the water, and Coach blew her whistle to start.

And the most incredible experience of my short life happened.

I put my head in the water and pushed off the wall. I knew how to do a freestyle stroke—I just hadn't practiced it. A sense of calm assurance overcame me, like my body knew exactly what to do. I sped up, enjoying the regular sweeping motions of my arms and kicking my legs. In no time, my fingers brushed the far side. Astonished, I held on to the deck and looked down the pool. None of the other kids were even two-thirds of the way down, and several had turned around to head back to the start. Dawn rested at the halfway point, watching me with huge eyes, one arm draped over the lane markers. Coach stood on the pool deck five feet away from me, staring at me with her mouth open.

By the end of the first week, I moved ahead a class, which practiced at a different time. Dawn pouted as she said goodbye, but she didn't try to stop me. By the end of the summer, I was swimming with kids three years older than me. And beating them.

I'd found what I was born to do.

By the time I was a freshman in high school, no one in the school could keep up with me. My senior year, I beat everyone in the *state*.

And I owed it all to Dawn. Without her, I never would have gone that first day.

But the teasing and bullying didn't magically go away. In fact, it got worse for a while as the gang realized I was much better than them at something. I put my head down and persevered. I was still the gangly, skinny kid, and some of them were much bigger. But by the time I was a sophomore in high school, my former tormentors held me in a sort of wary awe. One of them tried his luck with me that year. I only needed a few punches, and no one bothered me after that.

But it was still hard not to see myself as that gangly, skinny kid.

Next to me, Dawn stretched her arms out sideways on the pool deck. "We might have started swimming together, but something tells me you would have found your way to it eventually. You're too good for that not to show up at some point."

"Maybe. But I'm still glad it was you who nudged me into it."

She tipped her head toward me and gave me a private smile that nearly stopped my heart. "Me too. I love bragging about you."

"You need to find something better to brag about then. Set your sights a little higher, Dawn."

"You sure are bossy all of a sudden. Barging in on my vacation and now telling me what to do."

I smiled but remained quiet.

She sighed. "But I'll take the bait if you want to change the subject. How about this—who knew Pure Sands being a dump would turn out to be such a good thing?"

I laughed softly. "I've got to admit, this is pretty sweet."

"I'm really looking forward to Ubud tomorrow. It's the artistic center of Bali. All kinds of artisans, and the town is supposed to be gorgeous. We're going to see the surrounding area too." She leaned forward to watch me. "Is there anything specific you want to do on this trip?"

Several answers to that question popped into my head, each more inappropriate than the previous. *Lift you out of the water and lose myself between your legs. Pound into you until you scream my name.*

I owed Dawn so much, and I knew her question was an honest one she wanted an answer to. "I want to dive some more."

"That's easily enough arranged. And I knew it—you only want to get better at it than me."

I rolled my head on my neck to stare at her, then pinched my fingers and drew them across my lips, zipping them shut.

We both laughed, the easy laughter of life-long friends. I was happy with whatever we did. As long as Dawn and I were together, nothing else mattered. And even if I wanted to be more than that, was it worth risking everything we had now? I submerged and pushed off the wall, swimming the length of the pool. Maybe a little distance would give me some clarity to answer that question. Because I didn't have a clue what I wanted.

Chapter Seven

Dawn

I OPENED MY EYES, and it was dark. Again.

I lay on my side but didn't have that comfortable, woozy feeling like I could go right back to sleep despite the solid, comforting warmth cocooning me.

Wait. What?

Thoughts of checking the time fled as I realized Cole had wrapped himself behind me, bending his long legs behind my knees. His breathing was deep and regular behind my ear, so I had no doubt he'd snuggled up to me in his sleep. A smile tugged at my lips as his hand twitched— the hand that lay on my hip. He'd worn the same pajama bottoms to bed, once again forgoing the shirt. Behind my back, his bare torso was soft and yet hard at the same time.

If I hadn't been wide awake before, I sure was now. I longed to pull his arm across my chest and shimmy backward to get even closer. But that would undoubtedly wake him up, which might be a *little* embarrassing.

No, it was a better idea to keep this silent interlude my

little secret. Something to smile about and remember when I was down. I flicked my eyes to the bedside clock and discovered it was almost 5:00 a.m. So at least I had slept a little later this time. I didn't want any awkward exchanges if Cole woke up and discovered himself like this.

Especially the hot, rigid length pressed between us—a substantial length.

No, as much as I'd like to turn over and do something with that hot, rigid length, I was sure Cole would be horrified.

Stop fantasizing and get your ass out of bed!

At least my inner voice was thinking clearly, even if my body wasn't. As quietly as possible, I moved Cole's arm from my hip and scooched over to the side of the bed. He murmured and shifted position slightly but didn't wake up. I breathed a relieved sigh.

In the bathroom, I swapped out my tank top for a T-shirt, then quietly tiptoed across the room. Coffee could wait until Cole woke up. I opened the bungalow door and stepped outside. The early morning was silent except for the sound of the ocean meeting the shore. I climbed onto the daybed in the gazebo. The sky was lightening in the east, and the temperature was perfect for my choice of T-shirt and shorts.

Drawing my knees up, I looped my arms over them and rested my chin on top. A simple shrine lay near the path, a tall pillar with several openings. A woman had come by several times yesterday to leave offerings of flowers and incense. Remarkably at peace, I inhaled the rich, exotic scent that still permeated the air.

Half an hour later, the bungalow door opened and closed behind me, then Cole appeared with a steaming mug of coffee in each hand. Now wearing a T-shirt, he handed me a mug. "Good morning."

"Thanks for the coffee," I said quietly and moved over to make room. "Today we get to see more of Bali. Now that we're at Haven, we're going to have an amazing time. I can feel it."

He laughed, his eyes glittering in the growing light. "You always look on the bright side."

I took a sip of the sweet liquid—he'd made me the same variety I'd had the previous day. "I try to. Otherwise, it's too easy to drown in your own sorrows. And that's no good for anyone. If my marriage had worked out, I wouldn't be here right now. With you."

"I'm sorry—that your marriage didn't work out. I know how much a family means to you."

Cole understood me like no one else. He was so easy to talk to. "Thanks. I know Blake has never been your favorite person."

He hesitated before answering. "No, he isn't. But I never want to see you hurt."

Cole's and my friendship had been an issue with Blake from the beginning. Blake and I got together when we were freshmen at Cal State. Cole was in college half a country away, but we still talked and texted frequently. Blake hadn't liked that, though I'd done my best to reassure him we'd never been anything but friends. But as my relationship with Blake deepened, Cole and I gradually grew more distant, the phone calls eventually turning into infrequent texts.

Cole had attended our wedding, remaining polite and considerate even when Blake made cutting comments about fish that got away. That was when Cole's opinion of him solidified into deep dislike.

And he was right, wasn't he? Blake tried to blame me for what happened but couldn't face up to his own fault in our breakup.

"I'm better off without him. I see that now, though it took a while to get to this point." I clinked my coffee mug to his. "Thanks for coming home to rescue me."

"You didn't need rescuing. You just needed a friend. And when Coach Terry called with the offer to sell me Iron Horse Gym, everything came together. Like it was meant to be."

Nine months ago, I had been stuck in a deep funk involving endless containers of Ben and Jerry's, along with the Cure on repeat. The divorce was almost final, and Cole was worried about me, calling or texting almost daily to check in. When he announced his high school swim team coach wanted to retire and had offered to sell Cole his gym —the gym where Cole had spent his formative years—I'd finally seen a glimmer of hope.

Cole moved back to San Bernadino, and I pulled myself out of my misery, rededicating my energy to teaching and my kids at school. "Terry wasn't upset when you wanted the time off to come here?"

Cole shook his head. "It was good timing. He's ready to hang it up, and this gives me a nice break before I have to jump into the deep end."

"You'll do great. And that exercise physiology degree should come in handy."

He grinned and took a sip of coffee. "Yeah, it's a great gym. Too bad it doesn't have a pool. Maybe someday I can figure out how to build one. What about you? Are you going to start back on your master's degree after we get home?"

I had been able to get a job without a master's in education through a special California pilot program, but I was expected to earn it eventually. I'd been making solid progress until things got too awful with Blake. I hadn't opened a book since I left him, but now I nodded. "Definitely. I'm three-quarters of the way there, and it's time to finish what I started. Plus, the school district will pick up most of the tab."

Part of the reason we'd hurried to take this trip was because school would be starting a week after we returned. Then it would be nearly impossible for me to get the time off.

"I'm glad to hear that." He took my empty mug and moved to the side of the gazebo. "Shall we get this day started? We've got an island to discover."

Our car wound over a narrow road with rice fields on both sides. Haven had provided a private car and driver to help us explore. Next to me, Cole placed both hands behind his head and stretched. "That was great. I've never seen rice terraces up close like that."

"Those mountains were so steep! I can see how terracing the field would be the only way to grow a crop."

We were heading toward the town of Ubud after visiting a steep valley terraced with orderly rows of impossibly green rice. Palm trees were left where they had grown naturally, providing shade for workers.

"It hardly looked real," I said, then craned my head out the window. We traveled down a long hill and through an underpass, the sides of which were constructed of stamped blocks of concrete. That wasn't what caught my attention. The entire structure was covered in a long green carpet of vines.

Cole blew a low whistle. "This place keeps getting better and better."

After another ten minutes, our driver pulled over on a busy street and smiled in his rearview mirror. "This is central Ubud. I'll be back to pick you up here at two p.m. That okay?"

"Sounds perfect," I said, and we exited the car. We walked along the sidewalk, which was busy with a mixture of tourists and locals. Shops selling hand-crafted wares, yoga supplies, as well as a broad selection of restaurants lined each side.

As we passed a shop with the delicious scent of coffee wafting out, Cole gasped and screeched to a halt. "They make luwak coffee! Let's try some."

I groaned. Being a fan of Bali, I was familiar with the drink. "Cole! Yuck. You really want to drink that?"

He scowled at me. "Look, I let you off the hook with the exotic dinner, so the least you can do is drink a cup of coffee."

Knowing a losing battle when I saw one, I reluctantly agreed. "All right. One cup. And I'm only doing it for you."

Cole broke into a sunny smile that made me laugh despite myself.

"You have to admit it smells great," he said, turning toward the shop. "Let's go."

Chapter Eight

Dawn

WITH TREPIDATION BUILDING STEADILY, Cole ushered me through the open door ahead of him, where a young man in dark pants, a white tunic, and brown udeng greeted us.

"We want to try luwak coffee," Cole said from behind me.

"Of course," the man replied with a small bow. "Would you like a tour that shows how the coffee is made?"

I thought this was a case of ignorance being bliss, but stiffened my spine. "We'd love that," I said sweetly, then shot Cole a dirty look.

He grinned back as our guide, who introduced himself as Ketut, led us to a floor-to-ceiling enclosure, the front covered with a panel of glass. A gnarled tree decorated the inside, along with several wooden turned-over boxes, holes sawed in the end. A carpet of leaves lay over the floor. A brown, weasel-like creature dug a group of leaves into a pile while another snoozed on a branch where it met the trunk of the tree. The second was light gray in color, and both had long tails.

"These are luwaks," the man said and pointed to a stainless-steel dish of coffee beans next to a water bowl in the corner. "We feed them raw coffee beans, which they often swallow whole. The luwak then digests the beans, and we collect the end… result."

I swallowed hard, trying to ignore Cole's grin.

"Do you, uh, wash the result?" I asked.

Ketut broke into a broad smile. "Oh, yes. Don't worry. Let's move on."

We passed into an open area. A woman stood over a wire mesh screen, running a streaming hose over it and the small brown nuggets on top. The water emptied through a drain in the floor.

"The luwak's excrement gets washed away, leaving only the processed beans," Ketut said. His English was formal but very correct and easy to understand. "We collect those, then dry them. Next, all are roasted by hand." He led us through a door into a small, hot room. A rich, heady scent met my nose, and for the first time, I entertained the thought this coffee might be drinkable after all.

Despite its origins.

An open, circular firepit dominated the center of the room, where several people held wooden paddles over the flame. Coffee beans were roasting on the wooden surface, with the workers expertly shaking them every few minutes to keep them from scorching.

Ketut stopped next to the firepit and faced us. "After the beans are roasted, we let them rest for several days to fully develop the flavor. We separate some to sell as whole bean coffee and grind the rest—the final step in the process. Come this way."

We followed him out the door and into a cozy room with a long bar on one side. Several tables were placed around the café. Ketut slid behind the counter and lay two menus before us. "We sell both pure luwak coffee as well as a blend mixed with natural coffee grown near Ubud. As you can see, luwak coffee is a very laborious process, which is why it is so expensive."

The prices were in US dollars. I gasped to see the pure luwak coffee was forty dollars a brewed cup.

Ketut saw my reaction. "I would also like to point out we aren't the least expensive brewer in Bali. This is by choice. Our luwaks are kept in natural, humane conditions and our farm is inspected regularly." He nodded across the room at the glass enclosure where we had started our tour. "The animals kept here at the café are rotated regularly to keep them from becoming stressed."

I nodded, feeling better that the animals were treated well. Some luwak coffee farms were on a similar level as puppy farms. But forty dollars!

"We'll take two pure coffees," Cole said, plucking the menu out of my hand and handing both back to Ketut. I was opening my mouth to protest that a blend would be fine when he shook his head. "I'm buying. We'll never get another chance. I'm not letting you chicken out on me. Or get cheap."

I laughed, knowing he had me pegged. "Okay, fine. Weasel-poop coffee, here I come. If I get sick, you're responsible."

"You won't get sick."

We took our brewed coffees to a table in the corner and sat down. I even refrained from adding cream or sugar, just to make sure I got the full experience. I had to admit the coffee had a rich, aromatic scent.

Here goes nothing.

I lifted the porcelain cup to my lips and drank a healthy sip. The taste was earthy and thick, definitely different than other coffees I'd had. But there was no denying it wasn't bad at all. "Okay, I might actually be able to drink this. There's a solid chance I'm going to live."

Cole winked at me. "See? Told you so."

I took another long drink, then stared at the dark brown liquid, considering its implications. I sighed. "You're right, though. I feel like I'm afraid to take the smallest risks anymore. Like I've lost all my confidence."

He snapped his head up. "I never said that!"

"You didn't need to. That's what this trip is about. And thanks for nagging me into trying this."

"You're welcome." He held up his cup in a toast, then took a long drink.

"I am *not* eating bugs or drinking blood, though."

Cole laughed. "Baby steps. We've still got lots of time left."

"You've always been the adventurous one. Willing to prove yourself."

A shadow crossed his face. "I had to prove myself."

"I know." I spoke gently, my heart twisting at the memories. "You had it pretty rough as a kid. You sure showed them in the end, though, didn't you?"

"Maybe. I'm not sure."

I laughed, wanting to break him out of this sudden mood change. "I remember when you went to that swim camp the summer you were thirteen. I hardly recognized you when you came back!"

A begrudging smile rose on his face. "Yeah, they could hardly keep me fed. I think I grew over six inches that year.

That was when I discovered weights too, and finally started to pack on some muscle."

He wore a sleeveless shirt and as he lifted his arm to take another sip, I couldn't help noticing the muscles flex in his upper arm. Not to mention the two tattoos he had on his left one. The yellowish disc on the outer side of his bicep, and the other tattoo on the inside—the one he had placed there so it would always be close to his heart.

I finished my cup and placed it back on the saucer. "And look at you now."

He met my eyes steadily. "Sometimes I still see myself as that tall, skinny kid who got picked on all the time."

I reached across and took his hand. "I know you do. Despite all evidence to the contrary."

A shiver ran through me as Cole brushed his thumb over the back of my hand. Something changed in his eyes, and my breath caught. Our eyes held, and I was intensely aware of the feel of his thumb over my skin. He dropped his gaze to my mouth before raising it again. I leaned forward slightly, our hands still together.

Raw craving burned in his eyes. I had to be imagining that!

I remembered the feeling of him behind me that morning—especially *that* part of him. Heat spread like lava through my abdomen. But Cole could have any woman he wanted. The last thing he needed was a hot mess like me. Then the flicker of desire left his gaze, and I wondered even more if I'd imagined it.

He squeezed my hand and withdrew his. "So back to diving tomorrow?"

I blinked, bringing myself out of the spell. "Yes. I can't wait. I was proud of myself for passing my certification, but I'm honestly shocked at how well I did yesterday."

"You only need to get your confidence back. You're one of the most unstoppable people I've ever met, Dawn"

"Hardly. But I'm trying. Sometimes you have to get some distance from a situation before you can get perspective on it. Blake really did a number on me mentally. He convinced me our failure to get pregnant was my fault—that there was something wrong with me." I breathed a long sigh. That accusation was a mountain I'd yet to climb. "Finally, I couldn't take it anymore and had to leave for my own sake."

"I really regret that we grew apart over the past few years. You needed a good friend, and I wasn't there."

"You know why I stopped contacting you."

Cole's shoulders tightened. "Blake. Another reason I can't stand that guy."

"Thanks. You had plenty on your plate too—and I wasn't there to support you, either."

"You were when it counted."

I forced a smile. "I would have loved to tour all those sights in Barcelona with you. Such a beautiful city."

He snorted. "I hardly saw them."

I winked at him, then became serious again. It was confession time. "You know what prompted me to go on this trip? Specifically?"

Cole shook his head.

"I finally took a long, hard look in the mirror. At what I was doing to myself—the misery and guilt. And I pulled myself up by my proverbial bootstraps. I decided right then and there I was done with the grieving—Blake did me a huge favor. Now I'm free. That same day, I got the email about the Bali trip. I don't think that was a coincidence. I believe it was fate."

"It is fate," he said quietly.

"I need to come to grips with what happened, and what may or may not happen in my future. This is the start of that." I swallowed over the lump in my throat.

"You deserve so much better than him."

"You're right. I do!" I smiled, but it faltered at the look on his face. There was sadness there, and something else. The same thing I'd glimpsed before. The sadness made sense—I knew he felt bad for what I'd gone through. And I was probably so screwed up I was imagining the desire. The hunger.

No doubt I was projecting my own desires onto him. Maybe I did deserve better than Blake. But Cole surely deserved better than me.

Chapter Nine

Cole

THE NEXT AFTERNOON, I rifled through my T-shirts in the closet, then simply picked one at random. I didn't need to dress up to hang out at the main resort pool.

Dawn dug through her mostly empty suitcase before rising with a frown. "I can't find my sunscreen. Do you have an extra tube?"

I slipped into my flip-flops and pointed with my chin. "Yeah. In my suitcase. Help yourself."

She crossed to a corner and lifted the lid of my suitcase. I had just stuffed a paperback in my sling bag when I remembered. I froze, clenching my eyes shut.

Oh shit! Please don't look too closely.

I knew I was caught when she broke into guffaws. "Sunscreen's not the only thing you have in here."

Face already heating, I turned around to face the music. Dawn held my box of condoms in one hand, a giant smile on her face.

"I was a Boy Scout, you know. I like to be prepared."

She arched a brow. "I guess!"

Tapping my fingers on my hip, I tried to salvage the situation. "We had separate rooms reserved, remember?"

Dawn's sly smile fell. Not the reaction I was going for. Regret filled her face. "I'm sorry, Cole. I've screwed up your trip, haven't I? If you meet someone and want some alone time, let me know. I can hang out at the bar or something."

I rolled my eyes, trying to be nonchalant even as I instinctively shoved my hands in my pockets. "Nothing's screwed up! I'm much happier at Haven, okay? Can we please forget you found those, for God's sake?"

My obvious discomfort made her smile again. "All right. Do you want me to try to hook you up with someone?"

"Hell no!"

She laughed, and that made me happy despite the horribly awkward situation. She tossed the condoms back in my suitcase and closed the lid. "Consider it forgotten. Let's head to the pool."

"Hallelujah." *Now I really need to swim some laps.*

But the afternoon was much too beautiful to remain embarrassed, and my equilibrium was restored by the time we reached the big resort pool. Dawn and I walked across the flagstone pool deck, looking for two loungers to use. That wasn't a problem because we were the only ones there.

I scanned the serene area. "I can't believe no one's here, but I'll take it. Thanks for hanging out at the big pool with me. I know it's not as private as ours."

She spread out her towel and lowered the brim of her baseball hat. "This is perfect. There's more sun here, and I wanted to get a little bit. Swim all you want." She slathered on some sunscreen and didn't even smirk at me. My residual mortification finally faded. She pointed at my hips. "You must not be too serious about doing laps, though. You're wearing board shorts."

I stopped adjusting my goggles to eye her, deadpan. "I'm on vacation. The Speedos are all at home."

She cupped a hand behind her ear and scanned the empty area. "What's that sound? Oh, all the women around the resort crying."

I threw my towel at her and she caught it, breaking into lilting laughter. Not wanting to give her any more ammunition about hooking me up, I strolled to the deep end of the pool.

I'd tossed in the condoms at the last minute in case I made a connection with someone here. And now that wasn't even on my radar. I snuck a glance at Dawn. She wore a white bikini, and her skin had already developed a light tan. She was toned, yet curvy in all the right places. I was becoming more grateful for my baggy shorts with every second. I was generally so focused when I wore a Speedo that turning it into a banana hammock hadn't ever been a problem. But being around Dawn twenty-four hours a day was a new experience, and now I had another reason to be glad I'd left them behind.

I dove into the cool water and swam the length of the pool underwater. I could tell from the number of strokes that the pool was close to twenty yards long—good enough for laps. After taking a breath, I pushed off the wall and settled into an easy freestyle stroke, performing a flip turn when I reached the far end. Quickly, I settled into the back-and-forth rhythm so familiar to me.

Ten minutes later, I was warmed up and considering moving into a working pace. When I lifted my head to check on Dawn, Quinn and Steph, both in swimsuits, sat next to her on a lounger. All three of them were talking, which changed my plan.

Our dives that morning had been every bit as impressive as the first day's, and Quinn and Steph were the only others in our group. We dove the Liberty again, but Wayan took us to a different part of the ship, which made for a completely new experience. The second dive was on a sheer wall bursting with thriving corals. Every dive we'd had was sensory overload—it was hard to know where to look when wonders were everywhere. I closely watched Wayan and Quinn as they dived, and I was improving by leaps and bounds.

Now I swam over to the side of the pool and folded my arms on the deck. "Glad you guys came by."

Smiling, Quinn stood and stretched his arms over his head. "You're making me feel guilty. I haven't done much swimming since we've been here. Mind if I join you?"

"Not at all. Jump in."

Dawn grinned. "I wouldn't challenge him to a race, Quinn."

"You were moving pretty fast. I take it you swim a lot?" Quinn jumped in next to me, and we moved to the shallow end.

"Yeah," I said, not feeling like elaborating that he'd been watching my warmup pace.

We pushed off, and Quinn's swimming ability impressed me right off the bat. Almost immediately, he pulled ahead. I increased my arm turnover to pull even with him and we kept the same pace until we reached the deep end. He matched my flip turn and I smiled when he increased his speed again.

We still weren't going fast enough to make me breathe hard, and I had no desire to make the guy feel bad. God knows he was a better diver than I'd likely ever be. Everyone has their talents.

We continued for another fifteen minutes with Quinn slowly increasing his speed. I kept even with him but never pulled ahead, enjoying the companionship. We settled into a nice, fun pace, enough to stretch me out but not hard enough to make me really work.

I got into the zone and tuned him out. Swimming had always been a meditative experience for me. I completely lost myself when doing laps and was surprised the next time I lifted my head. I was by myself.

Pulling up, I glanced at the side of the pool where Quinn held on to the deck with one hand. Even from where I was, I could see his chest heaving. Dawn and Steph had both moved to sit at the end of their lounge chairs.

Dipping underwater, I swam across the pool and surfaced next to Quinn. "Sorry, I didn't notice you had stopped."

Quinn laughed, still breathing hard. "I get the feeling you could have kept on a while longer."

"Told you not to challenge him," Dawn said, waggling both brows and grinning gleefully. I ignored her, though warmth spread through my chest at her praise.

Quinn and I pushed ourselves out of the pool and I picked up a towel to dry my hair. Quinn joined me, dropping his eyes to my tattoo on the inside of my left bicep. "You're not even breathing hard! I'm guessing that tattoo has something to do with the clinic you just put on in the pool?"

I ran my index over the five interconnected rings. Two years after I'd gotten the tattoo, the different colors were still vivid. I shot him a crooked smile as I tossed my towel on the chair. "Like I said, I swim a lot."

Steph leaned forward, peering at my other tattoo on the outside of my bicep. "Wait a minute. Is that a gold medal?"

Dawn sat back on her lounger with a smug smile, obviously delighted to spill the beans. "Cole is biologically incapable of bragging, so I do it for him. You are looking at the two-hundred-meter freestyle champion from the Barcelona Olympics. And he got a second gold medal as part of the one-hundred-meter relay team."

"Congratulations," Quinn said, straightening as he shook my hand. "Though I'm not sure that's the correct thing to say. It's not like they gave you those medals."

I sat on my lounger, heat flushing over my face. Though immensely proud of my accomplishment, I was uncomfortable being praised like this. I glanced at my medal tattoo, a replica of the medals I'd earned in Barcelona but without the neck ribbon. Unless you looked closely, it could easily be mistaken for a generic medallion or large coin. "Thanks. When you compete in a sport that's measured to the hundredth of a second, there's a lot of luck involved."

Steph tapped her lip with one finger as she stared at the pool's surface. Then her eyes widened as she moved them to me. "I saw that race! The two hundred meters. You and another guy were in front—neck and neck. It was so exciting! I thought my heart was going to explode."

I grinned. "You're not the only one. I *barely* out-touched him. I've got freakishly long arms and hands the size of dinner plates. Another day, it easily could have gone the other way."

Steph smiled and patted Dawn's leg. "I see what you mean about him not liking to brag. You're the color of a tomato, Cole!"

Seems like the theme of the day.

I shrugged. It was impossible for me to explain why

swimming came so naturally to me. Why I could keep up a pace for an hour others couldn't match for twenty-five yards. I was born to swim.

Quinn moved to his lounger and lay down. "I didn't mean to end your laps. Don't stop on my account."

I settled back with a happy sigh. "That was plenty. I'm on vacation—I just wanted to get a few laps in. Though swimming doesn't seem to have crossed over too well to diving. Dawn's much better than me."

Quinn smiled. "You've already improved a lot. You're both comfortable in the water, which is the most important thing. You can't predict who's going to take to diving. I've had little old ladies dive the socks off pool rats." He turned to Dawn. "But Cole's right. You're a natural."

She leaned back with a laugh. "Aw, shucks. Thanks, it feels nice to be good at something. Even without the gold medals, this guy throws a pretty big shadow."

Dawn turned to me, and the pride and admiration in her eyes were so clear it brought a lump to my throat. I couldn't look away from her—she held me captive.

Yesterday, I'd come very close to either declaring I loved her or leaning over the table at the coffee shop to kiss her. Fortunately, I'd gotten hold of myself in time. Hopefully, I'd covered the sadness I'd felt pulling back from her. I'd handled a lot of rejection in my life—and had to press on when I'd rather curl into a ball and hide. But I couldn't face that crushing rebuff if it came from Dawn. Our relationship would never be the same.

I realized Steph had asked me something and wrenched my eyes away. "Sorry. What?"

"Are you training for the next Olympics? It's in two years, right?"

Shaking my head, I focused on the question, the spell

broken. "No. I've retired from competition. I wasn't expected to medal in Barcelona, let alone win. I peaked at the right time."

"You sure did," Quinn said. "I can't even imagine how much work must have gone into that."

I thought back to those long months—years—of training. And the small thing that had given me the spark to put my all into those races in Barcelona, especially the 200-meter individual final. One text had made all the difference. "It was a lot, which is part of the reason I hung it up. I'm in the process of buying my high school swim coach's gym. That won't be easy either, but I'm looking forward to it. Enough talking about me. How much longer do you two have?"

"We leave in three days," Steph said with a pout. "This morning was our last dive."

"Steph and I are going to a yoga class tomorrow," Dawn added with a nod to me. "Do you want to come?"

I smiled at the picture of me doing yoga. "No, thanks. I might be smooth in the water, but I'm sure yoga would be a different story."

"I hear you there." Quinn laughed and shared a private smile with Steph.

A server from the bar came by and I ordered a round of Bintangs for us. As I sat back with my cold bottle, sunrays sparkled on the pool. Amazing how water had carried me from a weak, willowy kid to the top of the Olympic podium. And then it led me back home to Dawn.

Out of the corner of my eye, I glanced at her as she read a book. The question was, where were she and I headed now?

Chapter Ten

Dawn

AFTER DINNER THAT EVENING, Cole and I took a dip in our private pool. The warm air caressed my skin as I stepped in. A nearly full moon hung overhead, and a soft breeze carried the scent of incense. I closed my eyes and inhaled deeply, wanting to trap the smell and the wonderful, calm happiness I was experiencing. "What a terrific day."

"Yeah, it was."

I wore my white bikini since it was still damp from this afternoon. Landscape lights shined on the bushes around the perimeter of our courtyard, providing dim illumination as I splashed around the pool. The water temperature was slightly cooler than the air, enough to be refreshing. Cole entered via the steps, dressed in only swim trunks, and the sight brought me back to the afternoon. He never brought up his accomplishments, and he'd purposely designed the tattoo of his gold medal to be vague enough that someone couldn't tell what it was unless they knew.

"I hope you don't mind that I told Steph and Quinn about your medals."

He smiled as he breast-stroked toward me, his handsome face pale in the moonlight. "No, it always comes out once I get to know someone. And we were at the pool, so my tattoos were on display."

Smiling, I shook my head. I settled against the side of the pool, leaning back against the tiled side. "Poor Quinn. He's a really good swimmer, but he had to stop and rest. You just kept chugging along."

"I was pretty in the zone—I didn't even realize he'd stopped. I lose myself when I swim, except during competitions. Then I'm really dialed in."

My smile faded. "That's one of the biggest regrets of my life."

Cole moved to my right side and slid down the wall of the pool. Only his shoulders and head were exposed to the air. "What is?"

"That I didn't come watch you in Barcelona."

"At the Olympics? I never expected that of you." His lined forehead broadcast his confusion, but knowing he was being completely honest didn't make me feel less guilty. It must have shown on my face because he continued. "You came to the Olympic trials. That meant everything to me. Though I've always had a feeling that caused some problems for you back home."

I closed my eyes and tipped my head back. "I missed the first trials you went to. I wasn't about to let it happen again."

He blew soft laughter. "You didn't miss much that first time. I was only twenty, so it was mostly for the experience. I was too young—not strong or skilled enough—to make a serious bid for the team."

"But it was the Olympic trials! I was head over heels for

Blake and he made it clear he wouldn't be happy with me going. I just wanted to please him. God, I regret that. There's so much I wish I could take back."

I took a deep breath and let it out slowly. There wasn't any need to protect my marriage any longer, and I certainly didn't owe my ex-husband any loyalty. "When I went for the Barcelona trials, Blake was furious with me. Before I left and after I came home. He was so jealous of you!"

"Even though he knew we were only friends?'

"Honestly, I'm not even sure his insecurity had anything to do with you and me specifically. He knew he couldn't measure up to you, and that ate him alive."

Cole narrowed his gaze on me. "I hope you didn't say that to him!"

"I didn't, but it's true. When I got back after you'd made the Olympic team, he was dead set on making me the villain in our relationship. He kept saying if I cared more about our marriage, we'd be parents by now. He laid such a guilt trip on me. I tried for the longest time to make it up to him. I walked on eggshells for months. A year ago, I couldn't take any more."

Cole moved in front to face me, placing a hand on my hip. I leaned into his comforting touch.

"I'm sorry," he said. "You never should have gone through any of that. I would have called him and told him he had nothing to worry about regarding us. Hell, you're the most loyal person I've ever met."

A nervous laugh escaped me. "I don't think you calling him would have helped the situation."

He placed his other hand on my opposite hip, a firm grasp to make sure he was getting through to me. "He was an idiot. And an asshole."

"No disagreement there. But I'm still sorry I wasn't there for you in Barcelona."

His hands resting on top of my bikini bottoms were comforting and slightly thrilling at the same time. As if we were balancing on a precipice.

Would we jump?

"You *were* there, even if it wasn't in person," Cole said. "You texted me every day."

"That was so incredible to watch! Local boy takes on the world and wins. And all you got from me was a phone call and some lame messages."

Darting his eyes to mine, an enigmatic smile rose on his face. He stroked both thumbs over my hips. "Your texts helped me push hard in every race. You'll never understand how much. Especially that two-hundred-meter individual final."

I looked into those hazel eyes, then studied his face. I'd been his friend for so long. Why hadn't I noticed his fine blade of a nose? His strong, masculine jaw? Cole was the rarest of creatures—gorgeous looks coupled with the biggest heart I'd ever known. "It was the biggest night of your life. And I wasn't there."

His eyes bored into me. "The biggest night of my life... so far."

I tipped my head back and smiled. "So far? You're gunning for something bigger than Olympic gold medalist, huh?"

"If I reach it, you'll be the first to know."

"Same here." I mirrored him, placing my hands on his slim hips, so my arms were inside his. There was a strong current between us, a new sensation. Electricity was flowing back and forth. I focused on his mouth, his slightly parted, generous lips. "I'm so glad to have you back in my life again. We've always been able to talk about anything. You know everything about me."

He lifted one hand from my hip and traced a finger over my collarbone. Slowly. Inch by inch. "Not everything."

His touch was featherlight, yet it ignited me like nothing I'd ever experienced. I inhaled deeply, all the blood in my body rushing to my center. We stared at each other, held in the moment. I couldn't have looked away if my life depended on it. His hand stopped, lightly resting slightly below my shoulder. Holding my gaze, his eyes were full of need and flush with desire. He was breathing much deeper than normal, as affected as I was. Yet he stood completely motionless.

And in that instant, I understood.

I hadn't been imagining his reaction yesterday. Cole did want me. But he would never go further than this—a questioning finger tracing along my collarbone. Especially with me being in my post-divorce, messed-up state. He was letting me make the decision, be in charge.

I felt like a blindfold had been ripped from my eyes and I was seeing clearly for the first time. Everything I'd ever wanted stood right in front of me.

But Cole needed me to make the first move.

I lifted my hand and stroked it across his hard pectoral muscle. The skin was smooth, hot, and hard under my fingertips. I had always admired him—he was a work of art, for God's sake. But to see Cole as *mine?* To touch anytime I wanted? This was heady stuff indeed. I fanned my fingers apart and drew them down the center of his chest. The raised ridges of his muscles danced beneath my touch, his chest moving back and forth with the force of his breathing.

He made a strangled moan in his throat, making me dart my eyes back to his. "What do you want, Dawn?"

Desire throbbed within me. I was no innocent virgin, but my experiences had never been anything like those depicted in movies and romance novels. I'd only had two lovers, and neither had filled me with passion. But I positively throbbed as I met Cole's eyes, now filled with raw hunger. Hunger for *me*. The knowledge was intoxicating, and I was on fire for him.

"I want you to kiss me, Cole."

He was a gentle giant. I expected him to lower his head and press his lips softly to mine in a romantic caress.

That wasn't what happened.

He rushed his hands to my ass and crushed me against him. I inhaled sharply, almost a gasp as a lightning bolt ran through me. Cole was so much taller than me and so much bigger. That was obvious as he ground his hips against me.

His lips met mine in a kiss that took possession of me. I gave myself freely, drowning in the sensation. Our mouths melded together, and he moved one hand to run it over the strands of my hair. He cupped the back of my head and claimed my mouth, probing deeply with his tongue. He was fire mixed with passion, and the surprise turned me on massively.

The electricity coursing through my body was a new experience. The pulsing. The *need*. Blake had never been overconcerned with my satisfaction, which hadn't filled me with confidence. I didn't exactly see myself as a sex goddess.

Tonight was different. Cole was bringing me to life. Bringing out the desire to lose myself... completely. To let him consume me. To lose myself, yet be completely safe at the same time.

I slid my hands up his broad back, tracing each contour with my fingertips. His skin was wet and slick from the water, the muscles hard and defined underneath.

How had I never longed for this?

I pushed my tongue into his mouth, circling that hot wetness. I wanted more. Much more. "Cole..."

"What?" He pushed the word against my lips.

I drove my hips against his, grinding against the rock-hard length of him. "Make love to me. Now."

Chapter Eleven

Dawn

COLE FROZE, every muscle becoming silent. His lips parted from mine, and his large liquid eyes held mine. "Are you sure about this?"

I pressed his palm against my breast and leaned into it. As he clutched his hand over my bikini top, jagged, electric sparks flew through me. "Very. Good thing you brought those condoms."

He twitched the side of his mouth, but only for an instant. His usual humor was gone—Cole was intent on only one thing now.

Me.

He pulled me toward him, and our lips met again, a joining of hot, wet flesh. Parting my lips with his tongue, he danced it around the inside of my mouth. My knees nearly buckled.

Where did he learn to kiss like this?

I had to bite back a laugh. He was literally making me giddy. I slid my hands up his torso and gripped both pecs.

They were larger than my hands and solid beneath my touch.

Cole moved his hand from my breast, up my collarbone, and around my neck. With one tug, he untied the bikini string around my neck, then the other around my back. The white fabric came free in his hand, and he tossed it aside.

Then, in one firm motion, he moved his hands to my hips and boosted me up to sit on the edge of the pool. He parted my legs and stepped between them, crouching slightly. Then he grasped my bare breast with one enormous hand and lifted it to his mouth. As he sucked in the hard peak, I moaned.

He swirled his tongue, moving his hand to my other breast and rubbing this thumb over it. With a gasp, I dropped my head back. The sky above us was lit with a million stars as the moon shined down on us. The warm scent of incense blended with the plumeria blossoms. I was drunk, but not with alcohol.

Pulses ran through my body, and I was panting more than breathing. Cole moved both hands to my shoulders and gently pushed me backward until my back contacted the stone pavers. Now the smell of the grass between them added its heady scent to the potent air. He kissed my stomach, stopping to swirl his tongue around my navel. A soft breeze tickled my wet skin, making me groan as I ruffled my hands through his short hair.

"Cole... I feel like I'm going to ignite. Right here."

He lifted his eyes, a ghost of a smile appearing. "I don't think so. But you will."

Moving both hands to my hips, he pulled my bikini bottoms down my thighs. Then he straightened to pull them off altogether. He dropped them to float on the surface of the pool near my top.

Then he stood squarely and became still. Nothing moved but his eyes, slowly taking in my naked body.

I swallowed but didn't move, slightly self-conscious at being exposed like this. Cole still stood between my knees, so my legs were spread. But his eyes told me I didn't need to cover up. He blew out a long sigh and brushed one hand across my stomach. "You are so perfect. You're gorgeous, Dawn."

He still wore board shorts, which was something I needed to take care of. Quickly. I sat up and reached for his waist, but he trapped my arm in one hand. His eyes blazed into mine, and his firm grasp on my arm sent heat rocketing through me. "Not yet," he breathed. "Lie back down again."

This commanding, assured Cole turned me on so much I didn't question him. I rolled back down as he bent over me. He returned to my breasts, grasping both of my hips firmly. Adjusting his stance, he drew a wet line to my navel.

And I started to worry, my confidence withering.

He couldn't possibly...

When he crouched and pressed another kiss to my lower belly, I had to act. My heart pounded in my ears, but now nervousness overcame the desire. "Cole, what are you doing?"

He looked up from my abdomen and raised a brow. "Exactly what it looks like."

Panic flooded through me, and I bolted upright. "You can't! We're outside!"

He drew his brows together, but a smile rose. "We're inside eight-foot walls, Dawn. We couldn't get more private."

"Yes, we can. Inside." Anything to distract him. "Besides, the condoms are in your suitcase."

He stared at me, trying to figure me out. Then he shrugged. "Okay. Let's go inside."

While we were at dinner, housekeeping had performed the turndown, and the room was softly lit. The mosquito net was drawn over the bed. Cole padded to his suitcase and retrieved the box of condoms. He lifted the net and tossed them on his nightstand. I followed him, watching the muscles of his back work as he moved. The romantic atmosphere and this gorgeous man in front of me brought my arousal roaring back.

When he straightened, I slid my arms around his waist and kissed his back. "You are the most beautifully built man I've ever seen."

He snorted quietly and turned around in my arms. "If you say so."

"I absolutely do."

The golden light in the room highlighted his chest and all the muscles in his abdomen. I ran my finger over his wet skin, making his abs dance. Stepping forward, I kissed the center of his chest. I swirled my tongue, tasting him for the first time. Eager now, I unbuttoned his shorts and slid my hand beneath. I grasped him in a firm hold, slightly shocked.

God, will the condom even fit?

Once again, passion was making me silly, and I was sure he would *not* appreciate me laughing at this moment. I dropped to my knees and pushed his shorts to his feet. He kicked them off. Grasping him with both hands, my mouth enveloped him. A deep, guttural groan escaped from his throat. I was fully confident again. *This* was something I was good at.

Cole gently held my head between his hands, caressing my hair. After only a minute or two, he inhaled a giant breath through his nose and stepped back. "Come here. Right now." Grasping my arms, he lifted me to my feet and kissed me.

Hard.

So hard our teeth scraped over each other's, and I had to take a step back to keep my balance.

I slid my hands to his bare ass and drove us together, feeling every inch where our wet skin came together. Feeling *him*, between us. Cole grabbed a handful of my hair and pulled my head back. "You need to get in that bed. Now."

I smiled, dizzy at this authoritative, confident Cole. "Or what?"

"Or I'll toss you over my shoulder and climb in anyway."

I kept the smile but complied, well aware he would have no difficulty whatsoever doing exactly that. Parting the mosquito net, I climbed through and slid under the covers. The white sheets were smooth and cool against my torrid skin. Cole followed but ripped the covers down to the foot of the bed. He settled on top of me, once more claiming my mouth with his. He thrust his tongue into my mouth, then just as quickly withdrew it.

He grunted hard, then rose to his elbows and rushed his way down my upper chest, only stopping to roll a slow circle over my breast. When he reached my navel, he pressed my legs apart, settling between them.

My heart hammered, embarrassment rising again. I swallowed—my throat was suddenly dry. "Cole."

He looked up.

"Are you going to... um?"

His expression changed, becoming guarded as he realized I'd stopped him in this same position at the pool. "I was planning to, yes. Don't you like it?"

I was glad the light was dim as heat flooded over my skin. Pretty sure the soles of my feet were blushing. "Uh... I'm not sure."

Cole stilled, then his forehead smoothed. "Wait a minute. Are you saying you've never...? No man has gone down on you?"

I clenched my eyes shut. "I've never been so embarrassed in my life. Forget it."

The mattress shifted and I opened my eyes to find him climbing back up. He settled on one elbow and stroked my face with his free hand. "No, I won't forget it."

"I want you inside me, okay?"

He placed his hand between my breasts, and I could see it moving from my pounding heart. "I want what you want, Dawn. But I think I'm missing something here. Don't you want me to?"

I forced out a shaky exhale. "I really don't want to talk about my marriage right now. Let's say I was told that act is gross and nasty."

Cole tightened his jaw, his eyes becoming stony before he closed them. He took a deep breath, then lowered to kiss me with incredible tenderness, a soft, feathery brushing of lips. It was like a golden beam of light warming my tiny, embarrassed heart. He kissed his way to my ear. "I don't think it's gross or nasty. And right now, I want to taste every inch of your body. Especially that part."

He lifted up to watch me.

"Only if you want to."

"What did I just say?" His voice was soft and gentle, completely opposite the authoritative tone he'd used only minutes ago.

"Okay. I want you to." My voice cracked and I swallowed again.

Cole kissed the tip of my nose. "I need you to do something for me."

"What?"

He pressed his lips to the corner of my mouth. "I want you to close your eyes and not think about a thing. Unless you want to watch me—that's a turn-on. Let yourself *feel*, Dawn. I promise I'll make it worth it to you."

"I believe you."

He lifted to meet my gaze. "Do you trust me?"

I smiled, and my nerves fled. "With my life."

"Then relax. And enjoy."

Cole kissed both my eyes closed, then whisked his tongue over my lips. I thought he'd scurry down my body and get to work, but he didn't. He stopped at my breast, rubbing the peak with his thumb until I moaned. Then he took it into his mouth, sucking and swirling.

I couldn't hold still, squirming with my eyes closed. I bit my lip, trying to stay quiet. A deep, regular pulse radiated from my core, getting stronger every second. He moved to my other breast, then drew a wet line across my stomach and ever downward. I ran my hands over his shoulders, breathing in soft gasps now. Every nerve in my body was electrified.

Cole ran his tongue down the crease where my thigh joined my body, and I jumped. The jolt rocketed through me.

Oh, yes. I was ready for this.

But apparently, Cole wasn't, because he moved to that soft crease on the other leg and ran his tongue up it, so slowly I was ready to scream. Then he blew a gentle stream of air over my sex with pursed lips. I arched my back, pressing my palms against the mattress as I cried out.

Then he moved in with his mouth. His tongue circled expertly, and I gripped the sheets with both fists. I had no problem taking his advice to relax and enjoy myself. I wasn't capable of conscious thought. My existence consisted of what he was doing to me with his mouth. And his fingers too.

I didn't even know what.

I didn't care.

I was dimly aware sounds were coming out of my mouth I had never uttered before. My climax was building rapidly. Cole gripped my hip with one large hand, holding me steady beneath him.

As the all-encompassing wave swept over me, a scream tore from my throat and I gripped his head with both hands, pressing him to me. My toes curled, my back arched, and my hands clenched, gripping his hair. My throat hurt.

Afterward, I couldn't even form complete sentences, but Cole apparently got the message because he slowly kissed his way up my body.

When he reached my breast, another jolt electrified me, and I cried his name into the still room.

He looked up at me and smiled. "Please tell me that wasn't your first orgasm."

I laughed weakly, glad I could talk again. "I've had orgasms, but that... was a first. I don't know what that was."

He kissed my breast again. This time the jolt was slightly less. Rising onto his hands and knees, he crawled across the bed to the nightstand and withdrew a condom from the box.

As he rolled it on, I stretched, reaching my arms across the bed. "I was worried the condom might not fit."

He raised both brows and smiled but didn't reply. Instead, he lay beside me and brought his lips to my neck. I traced my fingernails over his back, making him gasp, and his hot breath against my skin brought yet another shudder from me.

Shifting, he moved between my legs. "Is it all right if I kiss you?"

At first, I didn't understand why he was asking. Then I realized and grasped his head with both hands. I moved him to my lips, kissing him deeply and giving him no doubt of my reply. I was wanton with him. All traces of my self-consciousness and doubt were gone. He filled me with confidence, with the desire to do to him what he'd made me experience.

Reaching between us, he guided himself to my entrance then pushed inside. I inhaled as he filled me, stretching around him. Cole groaned, deep and throaty, then kissed me again as he started moving. I cradled his face in my hands and kissed him, gasping with each thrust.

"Oh my God, Dawn. I can't believe how good this feels." He pushed hard, sending another jolt through me, followed by a slow, building wave.

Again?

"Roll over," I whispered, and he turned us over. I sat up, straddling him as I ran my hands over every inch of his chest, then his abs. Moving up and down, I established a slow rhythm. Cole sat up, and we kissed as I rubbed my breasts against him. Both of us were sweaty and breathing hard. Our skin glided over each other's.

I groaned as I pushed my tongue into his mouth, wanting to taste all of it. All of him. He opened his eyes and watched me, a tiny smile forming. He drew one hand slowly across my hip and over my stomach, moving it between us.

"Oh my God!" I closed my eyes and rested my forehead against his, panting as I gave myself over completely to the rising sensations rolling through me.

Cole was breathing in gasps now, making deep, gruff sounds I'd never heard before. He wrapped an arm around me, pulling me tightly to him. I ground against his hand, moving faster and faster. Another climax rose within me, with Cole calling my name as I tightened my arms around him.

We held each other, both giving everything we had. For each other.

Chapter Twelve

Cole

I OPENED my eyes to bright daylight. Glancing at my watch, I wasn't surprised to find we had slept in—it was after eight. I glanced to my left. Dawn was still asleep, and the implications of what we'd done hit me full force.

Am I a complete dick for letting this happen? She hasn't exactly been in a good headspace since the divorce.

But she had been last night. She could have easily stopped me before we made love the second time. Let alone the third.

That thought brought a satisfied smile to my face, along with the increasing awareness that I'd woken up more than ready for round four. My mind might be worried about the effects of what we'd done, but my body was all for it. Dawn looked angelic in sleep—at peace. There was a line between her brows that hadn't been there a year ago. It was barely perceptible now. She deserved to wake up on her own, especially if she needed to process what last night meant.

I certainly did.

Quietly rolling out of bed, I pulled on my boxer briefs and crossed the room. A pile of energy bars lay on the desk, and I grabbed one as I quietly opened the glass bungalow door. I crossed to the table and took a seat, not seeing any need to be modest and put on my pajama bottoms and a shirt. Not after last night. Stretching out my legs, I rested my feet on the chair opposite and crossed one ankle above the other. Opening the wrapper, I took a big bite and chewed absently. Dawn had dedicated an entire section of her suitcase to a variety of snacks for me. I was always hungry, especially when in training, and she'd kept food around for me for as long as I could remember. Yet another reason I was crazy about her.

I stared absently at the pool, trying to decipher how I felt about last night.

I'd loved Dawn from afar for so long that I hardly knew how to feel. Physically, what we'd shared exceeded my wildest dreams and had been the most fulfilling, amazing sexual experience of my life.

But emotionally, it was a minefield.

A powerful sense of protectiveness washed over me, immediately followed by fury at Blake. I wanted to punch him for how he'd treated her. The embarrassed, bashful flush on her face at her confession about never receiving oral sex had made me determined to give her pleasure. But I wasn't sure she'd be able to relax enough to let it happen.

A slow, delicious wave of desire rolled through my abdomen.

Oh, yeah. She'd enjoyed *that*.

I had no doubt. And I got the sense it broke a mental logjam for her. She'd been a confident, willing lover after ward. Even taking charge the second time. The third time, I'd woken her in the early morning hours, and she'd turned to me. Warm, soft, and everything I'd ever dreamed of.

I tossed the empty wrapper on the table and rubbed my face with both hands.

But how would she feel about it in the bright morning light?

I'd been only her friend for so long, the role was comfortable—like a favorite pair of jeans. I never thought we'd be anything but friends.

Until we came on this trip.

And now that I'd had a taste of the forbidden fruit—literally—I wasn't sure I could go back. Of course, that wasn't Dawn's fault. If she didn't feel the same way about me, I'd have to figure out a way to deal with it.

Because the only thing worse than going back to the friend zone would be not being in her life at all.

The door opened behind me, and footsteps approached. Dawn set a tray on the table with the kettle boiling and our selection of coffee packets and cups ready to go. She wore her usual skimpy white tank top and terrycloth shorts. My heart took off, pounding against my ribs as I smiled at her. I tried to evaluate her mood without looking like I was checking her out.

"Good morning."

"Hello there, handsome."

She planted a kiss on the top of my head, which wasn't quite as good as the greeting I would've preferred. Namely, her straddling my lap, which brought back more memories of last night. But a kiss on the head was a hell of a lot better than tears, and my tense shoulders relaxed slightly.

In fact, she almost vibrated with energy as she lifted the

kettle. After handing me a cup of black instant coffee, she let her eyes take a slow, lazy vacation over my body. "Is it casual Friday already? I highly approve."

"Thanks for the coffee. And this is what I usually wear to bed."

She burst into a dazzling grin as she prepared her own coffee. "Hmmm. I don't recall seeing any underwear last night."

My heart returned to its normal slow thud as she took a seat adjacent to me. "I said usually... and last night was anything but usual."

"It certainly was."

She really seems okay.

Except I wasn't at all sure I was. Removing my feet from the chair, I sat up to face her. "Dawn, neither of us saw last night coming. I want to make sure you're all right."

As she sipped from her cup, she arched a brow over the rim. "Cole, I would think it was obvious last night to anyone who was paying attention that I was doing *all right*. And you were definitely paying attention. Expert attention."

Then the sly, satisfied grin fell off her face as she set the cup down with a clank. She bit her lip. "Are you okay? Do you... regret what we did?" Her voice was barely above a whisper and an artery throbbed in her neck.

Shit! She may not have been upset before, but she is now.

I reached out and took her hand, pressing it between both of my much larger ones. "Dawn, last night was one of the most incredible experiences of my life. This morning... I'm a little adrift. I feel like the earth's axis has tilted." *Be careful here. Don't scare her with a declaration of love.* "You and I—our friendship—has been one of the constants in my life. Now we need to figure out what happens now."

Her body tensed as she perched on the end of her chair. "You still think of us as friends? You don't want to be more?"

I want that more than anything on earth. "I want whatever's best for both of us. And I don't want to rush into anything you're not ready for."

She cocked her head. "The divorce was final months ago. Blake is totally out of my life."

But I learned last night he's still casting a dark shadow over you. I want to be more than your escape. "All I'm saying is maybe we should go slowly here. Think about this a little."

She twirled her mug on the table then lifted her gaze to survey the courtyard. "It is easy to be more than friends here. We don't have any responsibilities. We don't need to worry about how being a couple would work in real life. Home life."

I smiled and traced my finger over the back of her hand. "You're here to figure out who you are, remember? I don't want to complicate that."

"But what if who I am is tied to us being a couple?"

Oh, God. I sure hope so. "Then I imagine we'll come to realize that."

She nodded, but her bubbly effervescence was gone. Because of me. But I couldn't shake the feeling that she needed to think long and hard about what she wanted from life. And I didn't want to be an afterthought. Or worse, a crutch.

She laced her fingers through mine, and I held back tightly.

"I don't regret anything about last night, Dawn. But we need to make sure it stays that way."

"By letting things between us develop naturally. Makes

sense." She smiled, but it was shaky. "Thanks for being so concerned about me."

"I always will. Can I kiss you?"

Her smile strengthened. "Please."

I lifted a hand to her face and leaned in. Our lips came together in a long, soft kiss that held none of the frantic passion of last night. This kiss was more an acknowledgment that our relationship had changed in a fundamental way, but neither of us knew exactly what that meant.

At the same time, our lips parted, and we sat back in our seats. I took a drink of coffee, now lukewarm.

Dawn looked at her watch. "Wow, my yoga class is at nine. I need to get going. What are you going to do?"

"I think I'll head to the fitness center and lift for a while." Maybe weights would clear my mind.

"Do you really see yourself as that awkward, tall boy? Even now?"

I met her blue eyes. "Not all the time, and definitely not when they hung that gold medal around my neck. But yeah, it's been a struggle to overcome that. And the sons of bitches who made my life hell."

"Maybe I'm not the only one who needs to figure out who I am."

I smiled. "You're one hundred percent right there. That's one of the reasons I moved back home and bought the gym. To solidify my new Identity after retiring."

And to be closer to you, now that I wouldn't cause problems in your marriage.

"I'm sure you'll make it a big success. You've got the Midas touch, after all. Everything you work for turns to gold."

. . .

I SET down the forty-pound dumbbells and wiped my face with the towel, breathing hard. My normal weight routine took over two hours to complete, and I was less than halfway through. I'd finished three sets of hammer curls, and both of my biceps were twitching.

The layoff is showing.

Before we left for Bali, I had made working at Iron Horse my priority, neglecting my own workouts. I frowned, considering the gym's name. The Iron analogy was obvious, but I'd never been fond of the name, even when I'd been the gym's star member. It sounded like a place where a bunch of bros hung out, and that was *not* the image I wanted my facility to portray. I wanted the name of my gym to represent a goal everyone could identify with, but I hadn't come up with anything yet.

I moved to the leg press machine and my text tone dinged.

> Dawn: Steph invited me to have coffee with her and the yoga instructor. You mind if I go?

I smiled, not worried that Dawn was tiptoeing because of what had happened last night. She was always considerate.

> Cole: Go ahead. I've still got a lot of lifting to do.

> Dawn: Super. Maybe you and I can do something this afternoon? A tour or something?

> Cole: Sounds fun. You want me to look into it?

Dawn: Thanks. Now go show those
weights who's boss.

I SET my phone down and put my feet on the metal plate, preparing for my quads to burn. *I think today the weights are showing me who's boss, not the other way around.*

After taking a deep breath, I went to work.

Chapter Thirteen

Dawn

I SAT down at the restaurant table across from Steph. Yoga instructor Monica retied her curly dark-brown hair into a ponytail as she sat between us. All three of us ordered iced coffees and toasted over the table.

"Thanks for letting me crash your class," I said.

Monica, who was middle-aged with a refreshingly curvy shape, scoffed. "Now that the retreat is over, my schedule—and the classes—are more open. I'm glad you came."

I smiled at her sheepishly. "You made me feel welcome and not too out of place. Which is saying something since I'm not exactly a yoga expert."

"That doesn't matter." Monica had warm brown eyes and a calming, empathetic presence. "The important thing is whether you enjoyed it."

"I did." It wasn't a lie. The class had provided me with some alone time to process the sudden change in Cole's and my relationship.

Monica and Steph were friends and started talking about a place called Sandpiper Cay, which allowed my mind to wander. The yoga studio was near the fitness facility, and as we'd walked down the hall after our class, I'd peeked through the glass gym door. But I hadn't seen Cole.

That morning, I'd been on cloud nine when I woke up. When Cole wasn't in bed, I peeked out the front and saw him relaxing at the table. I put together what we needed for coffee and went out to greet him. Seeing him in only his underwear brought back memories of the incredible night we'd spent together. I'd never experienced anything that came close to the pleasure he'd brought out in me.

But the serious expression on his face as he stared at the pool changed my mind about the exuberant greeting I had planned to give him. Then, the more we talked, the more my mood changed.

Were we a couple? Hell if I knew.

"Dawn?" Steph asked.

I'd completely spaced out. "Sorry. What did you say?"

"I asked if you and Cole might want to do something with Quinn and me later today."

"Sounds good. I'm sure Cole wouldn't mind." He'd probably appreciate the buffer of being with another couple. Now my worry likely matched his. The more I thought about our problem, the more I hesitated.

Cole didn't have casual relationships. And my marriage broke up because of fertility problems. If we were a couple and got serious, was I being fair to him? He'd make a great father and could have anyone. Why would he want me?

"You've been pensive all morning," Steph said, setting her glass on the table. "Are you okay?"

I sighed and rubbed my forehead. "Sorry. I'm not sure, but you guys don't want to hear my problems."

Monica smiled sympathetically. "I don't have another class until after lunch, so I've got time."

"My whole morning is free," Steph said. "Quinn's touring the dive facility this morning. If you want to talk about it, we're here."

"Thanks. I could use a sounding board." I groaned and put my head in my hands. "I slept with Cole last night." Raising my eyes to gauge their reaction, I saw only confusion.

"And... that's a problem?" Monica asked.

"Considering we've been nothing more than friends for almost twenty years, yeah. It is."

Steph was raising her glass and set it back down with a loud thump. "You and Cole aren't a couple? I had no idea!"

I shook my head, then gave them an abbreviated account of our history, ending with the change of accommodations and single bed. "Since we're spending twenty-four hours a day together, things have changed."

"I can imagine!" Steph said, her face serious. "Sounds like last night wasn't... good?"

I tried to keep the laughter in but gave up, letting all the tension out. "Oh my God. It was the most amazing night of my life."

"But now you're scared this will screw up your friendship?" Monica asked, staring shrewdly at me.

"That's certainly part of it, but there's more." I leaned back in my chair, trying to put this into words. "I got divorced about six months ago. My ex was always jealous of my friendship with Cole, to the point that I distanced myself from him."

"Some men don't like their wives to have other male friends," Steph said with a shrug.

"Yeah, and I was committed to my marriage." I wasn't

going to get into the infertility problems. That was too raw and painful. "Cole and I dated other people in high school, then he got a full-ride scholarship to the University of Texas to swim for them. I went to college in San Bernadino and that's when I met Blake. We fell in love, and Cole was a thousand miles away. Then, when he was twenty, he went to the Olympic qualifying trials.

"The. Olympic. Trials.

"I told Blake I wanted to go, and he was really upset. We were engaged, so I made the choice not to go. And Cole didn't make the team. I felt awful about it—that I wasn't there to support him."

"That would be a hard choice to make," Monica said. "Did things settle down after that?"

"Yeah, kind of. Blake and I got married—Cole was there—but I knew our friendship would have to be reduced to occasional texts and holiday greetings."

It was a price I was willing to pay to reach my dream of a happy family, but it hadn't worked out that way. I took a long sip of my coffee, the smooth, cold taste chilling me as it went down. "Four years later, Cole went to the trials again. This time was different. He was more experienced and expected to contend. I couldn't miss that. Blake was against it, but I went anyway. And Cole made the team."

Steph reached out and held my hand. I was grateful for the support.

"When I returned home, Blake was furious, and money was tight anyway. He let me know traveling to the Olympics was out of the question. I'm a teacher and he's a salesman at a furniture store. I was caught between honoring my husband and my best friend, who was realizing a dream he'd worked his whole life for."

"You didn't go?" Monica asked.

I shook my head. "I chose my marriage. But things weren't the same between Blake and me after I went to the trials. Our fights got worse and worse, and I left him a year ago. It had nothing to do with Cole—we were never anything more than friends."

I traced my fingers over the surface of my phone, lying next to my cup. Then I lifted my eyes to Steph. "You mentioned watching Cole's Olympic two-hundred-meter race on television. So did I. Then I downloaded the footage to my phone so I could keep it. I was *so* proud of him! Over the past two years, I've watched it a lot, but something new happened after I left Blake."

I couldn't resist a small smile. The hard part of the story was over. "I'd watched that video probably a hundred times but never really noticed Cole as a man. He was just my best friend. During the live broadcast, I watched the race with my two girlfriends—Blake wanted nothing to do with it— and they positively *swooned* when they saw Cole. I rolled my eyes at them." I shared a laugh with Steph and Monica, feeling lighter at getting the raw, negative feelings out. "You know how during swimming races, they film the athletes coming from the ready room and out onto the pool deck? Then they introduce them?"

Steph and Monica both nodded.

"About ten months ago, I was really down one day, so I pulled up that video. The camera was filming Cole when he took off his robe and stood at the edge of the pool." I blinked several times, the image engraved on my brain. "It was like I'd never seen him before. He was... magnificent. He looked like something Michelangelo had carved! And I'd never noticed."

Monica breathed a blissful sigh. "I love watching men's swimming. It's my favorite sport in the Olympics."

All three of us laughed.

"Definitely," I continued. "That day, I watched the video over and over. Each time I paid more attention to *him*. To every second of that video. To his expression when he realized he'd won—the elation. The pride. I knew Cole like no one else. As he stood on the top of that podium, not only was he incredibly gorgeous, but he was the sweetest, kindest person I've ever met. And now that we're here at Haven, electricity has grown between us. Last night, the spark became a fire. And today neither of us knows what to do."

"From what you've described, he seems too busy to sleep around," Steph said. "It sounds like he's interested in *you*."

I thought of when I found the condoms, how mortified he'd been, and smiled. "No, Cole isn't a player. He had a girlfriend after the Olympics, but they broke up when he moved back to San Bernadino six months ago."

Monica cocked her head. "Because he wanted to be with you?"

"I don't think so. I've never asked, but I got the feeling the relationship had fizzled."

Though after what I experienced last night, how on earth could that happen? She was an idiot to let him go.

"Maybe you two should spend some time together instead of doing something with Quinn and me," Steph said.

I placed my elbow on the table and rested my chin in my palm, considering. "Actually, I think that might be a great idea. Cole and I can hang out together like we always have. Maybe that will bring some clarity."

Steph cradled her glass in both hands. "There's always friends with benefits."

I shook my head. "I don't think that would work for me, and I doubt Cole would be okay with it, either."

Monica finished her coffee and pushed it away. "Then it sounds like you'll have to let the situation play out over time. Leave it up to fate."

I nodded, but I was still troubled. Talking about our history only reminded me of what a fantastic man Cole was. And how he was my best friend in the world. Could I really risk that? And wouldn't he be better off in a relationship with someone other than me?

How could he not?

Chapter Fourteen

Cole

"HOW TECHNICAL IS THE TRAIL?" I asked the woman at the front desk. "Do we need to be good mountain bikers?"

She shook her head, smiling. "Oh, no! There are some ups and downs, but older children do this tour."

Quinn leaned on the counter and grinned at me. "If a kid can do it, hopefully, I won't fall on my butt too many times."

After my weight routine, I ran into Quinn, who had just finished a tour of the dive operation. When I explained I was heading to the lobby to set up a tour for that afternoon, he'd asked if Dawn and I wanted company.

The more, the merrier.

The buffer Quinn and Steph would provide might come in handy while Dawn and I danced around each other, so I readily agreed.

Now, we were nearly decided. "Can we do it on such short notice?" I asked the clerk.

"If you do a private tour with only four people, you can

leave at any time. Shall I call and see if they can pick you up in an hour?"

I exchanged a look with Quinn, who shrugged. "That works. The girls are having lunch now. That should give me plenty of time to grab a sandwich."

"Me too." I turned back to the front-desk clerk. "Go ahead and call them."

Five minutes later, we were booked. As I returned to our room, I grabbed a sandwich to go from the restaurant, noting Dawn and Steph were no longer there. When I entered the bungalow, Dawn sat in an armchair, reading.

"Hey. How were your yoga and lunch?"

She smiled at me, but her eyes were veiled. "Good. On both accounts. Did you figure anything out for this afternoon?"

"Yeah. I ran into Quinn, and he wanted to know if he and Steph could join us. I assumed that was okay with you, so we went up to the lobby together."

"Sure. I like them a lot, and Steph had a similar idea. What are we doing?"

"A mountain bike tour. We leave in an hour. Fifty minutes, actually." I sat across from her and unwrapped my sandwich before taking a big bite. Then I noticed Dawn hadn't responded. I swallowed, lifting my eyes. "Something wrong? I thought you'd enjoy a bike ride."

A red flush crept over her cheeks. "I would... normally."

"I made sure the tour isn't too gnarly. They said it's suitable for older kids." I took another bite. I'd eaten plenty of turkey sandwiches in my life, but this was *awesome*.

"It's not that, Cole."

I raised my brows at her as I chewed.

She pressed her lips tight together before blowing out a long breath. "I'm sore, okay?"

Swallowing, I thought about that. It didn't make sense. "You haven't worked out lately. Why would you be sore?"

She just stared at me, getting redder.

Then I got it and couldn't help laughing. "Oh! *That* kind of sore."

Flaming even redder, she nodded. "Yeah, that kind of sore. A bike seat might be a little uncomfortable. And stop laughing!"

I made a determined effort to rein it in. We were still on thin ice, and I didn't want to make things any more awkward. "Sorry. You want me to go up to the lobby and cancel? I can tell Quinn and Steph, too."

Her shoulders slumped as she shook her head. "No, let's go ahead. I'm sure I'll get used to it. Besides, Steph is sure to know exactly why I canceled. I don't want the embarrassment."

I cocked my head. "How would she know?"

Dawn winced, ducking her head as she looked at me from under her lashes. "Because I told her and Monica we slept together last night."

"Huh?" Then I sighed, eyeing the room at large. "Why do women always have to tell each other everything?"

"They knew something was up with me! I couldn't help it, and you know I'm incapable of lying."

As a kid, Dawn had been the worst liar ever, so she learned quickly that honesty was the best policy. I couldn't help a smile. "Yeah, I know. I'm sure Quinn knows now too."

"I'm sorry! I didn't mean to betray your confidence. I needed someone to talk to."

That hit home. She probably needed a woman's perspective. "It's fine. I'm not upset. Do you feel better after talking to them?"

She looked at her hands, twisting them in her lap. "I think so. Maybe. I'm still processing it."

"Me too." I decided to get back on safer ground. "So, you want to go ahead with the tour?"

"I do." Then she lifted her head, staring at me evenly. "But no snarky looks from you when we start or I'm putting a stick in your wheel spokes."

I laughed and held up my hands, pleased she was joking about it. "Deal. Let's get ready."

THE DIRT TRAIL was wide and well-groomed. We had two guides, one at the front of the group and another at the rear. A hot afternoon sun beat down, and even though it was slightly cooler under the jungle canopy, I was still pouring sweat. And very glad I'd worn a sleeveless technical-fabric shirt. I was the last of the four of us, with Dawn in front of me. She wasn't having any difficulties negotiating the terrain, but I would have kept an eye on her no matter what the circumstances.

Since I was the cause of her current circumstances, I watched her even more closely. Though that didn't stop me from breaking into a sly smile once or twice. If Steph had said anything to Quinn about us, he didn't show it. And neither did Steph—both treated us like they always had, which was a relief.

We biked over a mixture of deserted lanes and well-marked dirt trails. I'd been shocked to discover paved roads that weren't crawling with scooters and cars. We passed a massive temple complex, stopping at an entrance flanked by two carved stone monoliths at least twenty feet tall.

Next, we biked through a small Balinese village, peeking into the village temple complex as our lead guide explained about traditional Balinese life. We examined the temples from the outside—none of us was dressed appropriately enough to enter. As we biked down the village's main road, a group of children ran up to wave at us. Dawn waved back at a small girl, then we were past.

After the village, the track rose to travel along the crest of a ridge, beautiful emerald rice terraces or other crops on each side. The whole tour was unlike anything I'd ever experienced, and every time we stopped, I practically blew up my phone camera taking pictures. Once past the ridge, we entered the canopy again and turned broadly back toward the village.

Our lead guide Nyoman pulled over into a clearing and dismounted. In his mid-twenties, he explained he had attended a special school that taught English and skills for tourism. "We will stop here for a rest and some refreshments." He and the other guide produced soft drinks and Balinese sweet cakes wrapped in banana leaves from their backpacks.

After Dawn and I leaned our bikes against a couple of tree trunks, I bent down to murmur in her ear. "You feeling okay?"

She smiled and took a swig of Coke. "Yes, now it's my seat bones that hurt."

"I think all four of us might be sore after this."

"Nice to know I've got company." Her coy smile faltered. She unwrapped her cake and took a bite, turning away slightly.

My stomach lurched. While lifting that morning, preserving our friendship seemed like such an obvious idea. The safest, easiest route for us to take. But being in Dawn's presence made that very difficult. I was determined to give her as much time and space as she needed to figure out what she wanted from me—and the future.

But I wasn't sure I'd be able to look at her as only a friend again. Last night, one of my greatest dreams had come true. Today, I felt like I'd been rudely awakened, forced back into reality.

We strolled across the glade to where Quinn and Steph stood near the tree line. "You guys all packed to go home?" I asked.

Quinn waggled his hand in a so-so gesture. "The scuba gear is still drying out. It should be good to go by the time we get back. We'll be ready to go by tonight."

"I'm not sure about the ready to go part," Steph said before breathing a heavy sigh.

Quinn pressed his lips to her temple. "We've got plenty to look forward to when we get home."

"I know." She wrapped an arm around his waist and rested her head against his chest. Then she looked quizzically at Dawn. "Everything all right?"

Dawn's head was cocked, a faraway look in her eye. "Oh! Sorry, I thought I heard something. But now it's quiet." She focused on Steph. "Do you two have any other trips planned?"

"No," Steph replied. "But another guest here told us about a place on St. Croix that sounds great. We're putting it on our short list for sure."

"What's it called?" I asked, ever hopeful that Dawn and I would have another tropical adventure in the future.

Getting ahead of myself much? Let's get through this trip before planning the next one.

"Half Moon Bay Resort," Steph said. "It's a dive resort. I looked up their website, and the place is pretty cool. And much closer than Bali!"

"I'll have to bookmark the website," Dawn said. Then she furrowed her brow as she gazed toward the forest. "There it is again. Do you guys hear that?"

I listened but only heard birds singing. "What do you hear?"

"It sounds like a child crying."

Steph straightened. "I don't hear anything like that."

"Well, I do." Dawn turned her head, focusing hard now. "And it's coming from the jungle. Let's go." She marched toward the trees, and I followed.

"Should we get the guide?" Quinn asked, looking back at the two men standing on the far side of the clearing.

I looked over my shoulder at him. "Good idea. Why don't you get them and follow? But Dawn won't wait. If there's an upset kid out there, she'll find them."

She had already pulled ahead, so I trotted to catch up.

"Let me lead! At least I could move the branches out of the way."

"Can you hear the crying?"

I hesitated. I couldn't hear anything over the noise we made. "Well, no."

"I can. So I lead." She carefully stepped through thick branches.

I tried to keep an eye out. I was tall enough to see over her head, and I had no doubt whether she was hearing things. Dawn was like a bloodhound where children in danger were concerned.

After another twenty feet, I heard the crying too. Dawn picked up her pace, and now footsteps could be heard behind us—the rest of the group. We exited the trees into a small clearing dominated by a massive kapok tree, so big it had created a clearing below it. Its pale trunk rose toward the heavens, crowned with a halo of green leaves. A small girl with long black hair huddled within its giant roots.

"Stay here," Dawn threw over her shoulder. "I don't want to do anything to scare her."

I stopped as she moved forward in a crouch, a gentle smile on her face. "Hi, sweetie. Are you lost?"

She kneeled in front of the girl, who looked up, her face wet with tears. She looked around seven or eight and was dressed in jeans and a soccer jersey.

The rest of the group entered the clearing, and shock was plain in Nyoman's round eyes.

Dawn beckoned him. "I need you to translate. I think this is the girl I waved to in the village. Ask her if she's lost."

He hunkered down in front of the girl. A rapid-fire barrage of Indonesian ensued, then he turned to Dawn, who was next to him. "She's from the village. She was trying to follow us and got lost."

Dawn gasped. "Poor thing! That village has to be several miles away."

The guide shook his head. "We've circled around. It's no more than half a mile from here."

Dawn nodded, giving the girl another reassuring smile. The child smiled back.

"Tell her we'll take her back to her village."

The guide hesitated, looking back toward our bikes. "I'm not sure—we need to keep going. I can give her directions. I'm sure she can make it back on her own."

Uh-oh. Wrong thing to say. I stood back, waiting for the fireworks.

Dawn reached forward and gently wiped the girl's face dry, then spoke to the guide in a calm, sweet voice. "Let's go talk over by the trees." She patted the girl's hand and stood, holding her hand palm out to tell her to stay put. Then she grabbed Nyoman's arm and marched out of the child's hearing range.

I followed, reaching them as Dawn pointed a finger in the guide's face. "We are not leaving a small child alone in the jungle!" she hissed. "I'm taking her back to her village to make sure she's safe."

The guide shifted from foot to foot, clearly torn, so I spoke up. "I agree. We can't leave her here. We'll explain why we're late to your boss, so you don't get in trouble."

Dawn whipped her head to me, her eyes widening. I nodded to her. Given how focused she was on the girl, I wasn't surprised she didn't realize why the guide had been reluctant to vary the schedule. Nyoman was worried about losing his job.

She let go of his arm. "I can't just leave her here."

"I don't want to, either!" Nyoman looked on the verge of tears.

Quinn and Steph made their way over, the other guide behind them. "Why don't we all take her back?" Steph asked.

"I'm sure your supervisor won't be upset that you helped a lost little girl," I added.

None of us wanted to abandon a lost child, but Dawn leaving her was unthinkable. I recognized the firm set to her shoulders. Plus, every Balinese I'd come into contact with was kind and devoted to family. I was confident we could get the girl home and solidify our guides' jobs at the same time.

Nyoman straightened, giving us a firm nod. Then he spun around and headed back across the clearing.

Dawn looked up at me. "Would he really get fired for helping her?"

"I doubt it, but jobs are important. Especially on islands

that depend on tourism. When we get back to Haven, I'll call the tour company's office and explain the situation. It'll be fine."

After following Nyoman back, Dawn kneeled in front of the girl, taking her hand again as she spoke for Nyoman to translate.

After a few minutes, the guide nodded to Dawn. "She will go with us."

With a comforting smile, Dawn stood. She held out her hand and the small girl took it. Dawn kept a firm hold as they followed the guide down a faint path on the other side of the clearing.

AN HOUR LATER, we were still trying to leave the village as the reunited family tried to invite us all to dinner. The mother, still sniffling from time to time, clutched the child against her chest. The girl's absence had been noticed and we returned to a village alive with alarm. They were organizing a search party when we walked in with her.

Now the girl's father spoke to Dawn in broken English, indicating a small brick house nearby. Nyoman glanced at his watch and winced, then exchanged a long look with the other guide. I caught the gist of their unspoken conversation and got Nyoman's attention.

"Can you explain that we need to get back to our resort? We're honored to be invited to dinner but don't want to impose. We're very happy Rimba is safe."

Dawn had asked the girl's name on the hike back to the village. She'd held her hand the entire way and traded songs back and forth, hers in English and Rimba's in Indonesian. By the time we reached the village, the girl was smiling and laughing. And I wanted to wrap Dawn in my arms and never let her go.

After Nyoman translated my words, both Rimba's parents gave us the pressed hands bow, apparently satisfied we didn't think they lacked hospitality. All four of us returned the salutation, then the girl ran to Dawn and embraced her.

"Terima kasi," Rimba said, her voice small.

"Sama sama," Dawn replied with a smile and brushed her finger down the girl's small nose.

That brought a giggle, and Dawn stood again. We headed back to the faint jungle path, the entire village waving goodbye to us. I wrapped my arm around Dawn's shoulders, not caring that things might be different between us now.

I needed to touch her. The entire episode only brought into vivid detail why I loved her so much. She gave me a smile, but her eyes were hooded, hiding her feelings. The entire tour, she'd treated me the same as she always had. Like a friend. We walked side by side until the path narrowed, and I had to drop behind her. My side felt cold without her there.

But not as cold as our bed would feel tonight, with her so close and yet impossibly far away.

Chapter Fifteen

Dawn

I WAS A MESS. A massive, confused, conflicted mess.

After we returned to Haven, we said goodbye to Quinn and Steph, wishing them a safe journey home and promising to keep in touch with our new friends. Cole called the tour company to rave about our guides, and both he and Quinn tipped them lavishly.

Dinner was quiet and somewhat strained between me and Cole. The incident with Rimba only increased my dilemma about becoming a couple. During the meal, he told me several times how proud he was. That I took charge to help the child. He was trying to draw me into a conversation about it, but how could he understand? *I* didn't understand. Helping kids was part of my makeup, what filled my soul. So why couldn't I have one of my own?

All through dinner, the final fight I'd had with Blake ran through my head like some awful movie I couldn't turn off. I'd practically begged him to go to a fertility doctor so we could get some help. That only made him more furious, nastier.

Not much taller than me, Blake stared at me, his dark-brown eyes ice-cold. "I'm not going to any goddamn doctor to jerk off into a cup, Dawn. If there's something wrong between the two of us, it isn't me."

I was so stunned at his point-blank accusation, I couldn't even respond.

He scoffed and grabbed his jacket. "I'm heading to the bar. A beer is a lot better company than you these days."

I spent the night in our guest room, devastated. But sleep was elusive as a realization washed over me. How could I possibly want to bring a child into that environment? How could I think that a baby would solve the problems between Blake and me? He wanted a family too but had his own vision of that. One that only included his own biological child.

And he had no intention of compromising.

His blame cut me deep, exposing the fundamental differences between us. The ones I'd been blind to when I married him at age twenty: I was willing to work on our problems. He wasn't.

Blake made me question my worth as a woman, not just a wife.

I left him a week later, but the experience left me lost and shattered. If I couldn't be a mother, who was I? It was all I'd ever wanted. And seeing Rimba lost and alone brought all that guilt and desperate unhappiness back in force.

I'd come to Bali to find myself—my new self. Instead, all I had done was reinforce my old insecurities. I couldn't put any of this on Cole. He didn't deserve that. And he was the anchor holding me together right now. I couldn't risk our friendship.

We were quiet as we walked back to our bungalow. The bed was turned down and the mosquito net draped softly around it. I studied the scene. How could we have experienced such highs just last night? How could things have changed so much in only a day?

Cole slipped his sandals off and flopped into an armchair, raking his fingers through his hair. "Dawn, we have to talk about this. What's wrong? You should be proud of finding Rimba. None of the rest of us heard her crying. Only you. Yet, ever since it happened, you've built a huge wall around yourself."

I turned to him, to his imploring eyes full of pain and confusion, and eased into the chair opposite him. "Because it only highlighted that all I'll ever be able to do is help other people's children."

"You don't know that. Blake might be infertile! And just because he didn't want to adopt doesn't mean you won't ever have a chance with someone else."

I laughed weakly, but it faded at once. "What's the point? I'm so screwed up, Cole. I don't know what I want. I want a happy family with everything in my heart, and I'm not sure that will ever happen. I'd be as fulfilled adopting, but I'm too screwed up to even think about it. You're the best thing in my life, and I feel like that's in jeopardy right now. Losing you would be worse than the divorce."

"You're not going to lose me," he said softly. "You were always there for me when I needed you—I'll be there for you."

A tear rolled down my cheek. "You deserve so much better than me, Cole."

His foot bounced rhythmically, a sure sign of how upset

he was, yet his voice was quiet and beseeching. "Why? Why can't you see yourself the way I do?"

I managed a smile through the tears. "I could say the same about you. You're anything but a gangly, awkward boy. Yet you still see yourself that way. Maybe that's our fate—to be each other's mirror."

Pain flashed across his face before he covered it, though I wasn't sure why. "You're not broken, Dawn. But I can't make you believe that."

"I know." I moved my gaze to the other two armchairs, assessing the possibilities for sleep. They'd never work. "I'll sleep on the floor. You can have the bed."

Cole rose and went to the closet. He removed a spare blanket and pillow from the top shelf. "Don't do that. You can have it. I'll sleep on the bed in the gazebo outside. Good night."

And without another word, he left the bungalow, closing the door softly behind him.

Bending forward, I buried my face in both hands. I sobbed gut-twisting cries, trying to be quiet about it. Eventually, I wore myself out and climbed into bed. I brushed my hand over Cole's pillow, then gathered it to my face. It smelled of him—of raw sexiness and unselfish kindness in equal measure. How had I never noticed his scent before last night?

Last night had changed everything.

I wasn't sure we could close the gulf between us and go back to what we'd been. And he hadn't pushed to be a couple. He'd obviously enjoyed the sex—three times—but then he had withdrawn with the dawn. He said it was to protect me, but I honestly didn't know how Cole felt about me. How deeply he cared about me as a woman and not just a friend. Or a lover. He sounded as screwed up and lost as I was.

Weak morning light filtered through the closed blinds as I padded into the bathroom. I needed a moment to work up enough courage to face my reflection in the mirror. It wasn't a pretty sight. My face was puffy from crying and the bags under my eyes were dark like a football player's. Cole hadn't come back in during the night. Had I wanted him to?

Hell, yes!

His absence had left me feeling even more empty and alone. But the scared, lost woman in the mirror hadn't done anything about it. "What are you so afraid of?" I asked myself.

After my restless, miserable night, I knew the answer, even though I didn't want to admit it.

Rejection.

I don't think I could take it if Cole told me I wasn't enough. I looked into the mirror. "Why aren't I enough? I left Blake, not the other way around. Why do I think I'm the one with the problem!" I had doubted my worth as a woman. The other night, Cole helped me believe otherwise.

Helped me believe in myself.

The eyes in the mirror firmed, becoming decisive. More like *me*. I loved teaching. I loved my kids, and they loved me.

That was it. The answer.

I simply wanted to be enough. Exactly as I was.

My thoughts turned back to Cole. I wanted to be with him—completely with him. No one had ever understood me so well, and I doubted anyone ever would. How could they?

But I needed to know what he wanted.

"I need to know how he feels about me, and not only physically. About what we might be together. If we don't want the same things, it's better to find out now."

A sob escaped, my face crumpling in the mirror. "I *have* to know."

Spinning on my heel, I moved to the closet to dress. Then I left the bungalow with renewed purpose in my stride. And fear spiking in my stomach.

Chapter Sixteen

Cole

A LOW CLOUDBANK obscured the eastern horizon, giving a lurid crimson glow to the sunrise. After a long and fitful night, the red sky fit my mood. I sat up, piling the pillows behind my back. Every muscle protested at the movement, a reminder of yesterday's lifting session.

The pain was a welcome distraction from my mental turmoil. I needed to get into the pool this morning and work out some of this soreness. But the dull ache in my muscles was something I'd come to enjoy, even appreciate, over the years. In the growing light of the nascent dawn, I bent my arm and flexed. My bicep reluctantly contracted, and I acknowledged the truth of what Dawn had pointed out last night. I carried a lot of muscle, especially in my upper body.

So why did I still cling to the painful past?

I fluffed out my blanket before tucking it around me. I was plenty warm—the temperature inside the gazebo had remained comfortable all night. But I was out here, listening to crickets chirp, and not in bed holding Dawn in my arms like I should be.

I groaned, rubbing my hand over the scruff on my jaw. In my desire to protect Dawn and not jump into anything she wasn't ready for, I'd only made the entire situation worse.

She'd been a goddess in bed. After that shy, embarrassed beginning, she'd blossomed. I'd never experienced anything like what we'd shared together. What we'd become together. When she woke up yesterday morning, she'd been so happy she could have floated away.

Until I opened my big, fat mouth and made her doubt herself.

All day yesterday, she pulled farther and farther away from me. I thought the bike tour—and especially rescuing Rimba—would bring that positive energy back. If Dawn hadn't heard her crying, who knows how long the child would have been lost in the jungle.

I didn't understand any of it.

I only knew I was the cause.

My mind flashed back to when she'd said our fate was to be each other's mirror. A whole-body flinch wracked me, like it had when she'd uttered those words. I didn't want to be her mirror. I wanted to come home to her every night. I wanted to discuss our hopes and dreams—even more than we used to. I wanted to sleep next to her, listen to her scream my name in bed. Have a family with her. Hell, I didn't care if we had to adopt.

I stared at the bamboo and thatch ceiling, not really seeing it. "Yet I haven't said any of that. What do I have to lose at this point? Maybe it's time to be a man about this and speak the hell up."

And I *knew* I didn't imagine that connection between

us. We had been amazing together. But did she regret it? Was that why she pulled away?

It was becoming increasingly clear that I wouldn't be able to rest until I told her how I felt. The day was still young, but the sun was up now, an orange ball burning away the clouds and forecasting another sunny day. I'd give it a few more minutes, then go wake Dawn up if she was still asleep.

Movement and quiet voices distracted me from my musings. Three women climbed the short flight of steps from the beach onto the path. All balanced scuba tanks on their heads, and I recognized Wayan's wife Diah in the middle and his mother Melati in the back. From a conversation with Quinn, I knew dawn dives were popular, but I still felt a guilty pang at seeing the women working at the crack of dawn.

Then I saw something else.

Wayan's mother was lagging, moving stiffly with her face pinched and drawn. She stopped, rubbing both hands on the small of her back as she balanced the heavy tank on her head. I sat up, watching closely.

The bungalow was separated from the cement path by a lotus pond. The women walked right past with no idea I was there. Melati fell farther behind, and Diah turned around. She returned to the older woman, and the two women spoke. Diah looped her arm around her mother-in-law's, supporting her and urging her on while using her other arm to balance the tank on her own head. Even from where I lay, Melati's sharp, irritated response came through loud and clear. She waved off the younger woman, who resumed her march after a long stare. As soon as Diah turned around, Melati slouched, her posture radiating pain and fatigue.

Nope. I'm not going to stand by and watch this.

I put on my sandals. I still wore my shirt and shorts from yesterday, so I tossed aside the blanket and scooted to the end of the gazebo bed. Being tall has its advantages. I rose to my feet, and with one giant leap, cleared the pond and landed lightly on the cement path. I hurried to catch up to the women.

I hope I don't scare her to death, creeping up behind her like this.

The three women were small, but Melati was positively tiny, making me even more concerned about the weight she carried.

When I was a few feet behind her stiff form, I coughed politely. "Good morning."

Wayan's mother startled slightly, then placed both hands on her tank and moved to one side of the path. "Sorry, please..." Her accent was thick, uncertain. She indicated the path. "Go."

I shook my head and gave her my most reassuring smile. She didn't even reach my chest, and I didn't want to come across as some hulking monster.

Shit. How do I get her tank away without her losing face?

I indicated the scuba kit on her head. "Please. Can I carry the tank? I've always wanted to try that."

Melati's heavily lined brow became even more wrinkled as she stared at me.

I tried again, pointing to the tank. "Tank..." Then to my chest. "Me. Please."

Diah saw my pantomime and came back. "Is there... problem?"

Her English wasn't as proficient as her husband's, but she knew more of it than Melati. I screwed a big smile on my face. "I'd like to carry her tank. On my head, like you ladies do."

Diah cocked her head at me, obviously trying to make sense of my words. Melati hadn't had any qualms about telling her to get lost when she'd expressed concern, but I hoped I'd get a different reaction.

"You want... to... take her tank?" Diah's lined brow matched her mother-in-law's, though not quite as creased. Then it smoothed out. Her surprised eyes met mine before she gave Melati a shifty side-eye. The two women exchanged more rapid Indonesian.

Then Melati turned to look me up and down, her face blank with surprise.

I nodded helpfully, then got a surprise of my own when she burst out laughing. She waved an arm up and down my body as she talked to me in Indonesian, still balancing the kit expertly on her head. Evidently, she was explaining that guests didn't carry their own tanks, and I had a feeling men *definitely* didn't. But I didn't care if she thought I was an idiot. All I wanted was to get that tank off her head so she could get some rest.

Diah was drawing a breath to translate when I took matters into my own hands. Literally. I reached out and grabbed the tank from Melati, lifting it and placing it lengthwise on my own head. I was surprised at how much the damn thing hurt. It felt like daggers punching into my scalp.

How the hell does she do this?

Diah and the first woman in the line waved their arms frantically, calling out, "No, No!" while Melati only cackled harder. Eventually, she sobered enough to lift the cloth from her head. It was curled into a circle to make a platform, and she offered it to me. She had several missing teeth, which only made her smile more endearing. I snuck a peek at the other two women, who had similar arrangements between their heads and the tanks.

I was balancing the tank with one hand and already getting a headache. I didn't need any convincing. I slid my arm through the arm straps of the BCD and held it against one hip while I arranged the cloth platform on my head. After I got Melati's nod of approval, I returned the tank on top of my head. All three women burst into laughter. However, the new arrangement was much more comfortable.

But there was no way I could balance this thing without using my arms. These women were truly marvels.

All three women were still laughing. I grinned back, pleased with the response, and gestured for the lead woman to carry on. Then I held my elbow out to Melati and raised both brows. Still cackling, she looped her arm through, and we fell into line behind the other two.

Our small assemblage passed by the pool, and the front two women occasionally turned around to smile at me. With my neck getting steadily more sore, I smiled back and caught the extra gratitude in Diah's smile. Past where the patio ended, we descended a short flight of steps I'd never noticed. At the bottom, several picnic tables sat in the sand. Diah and the other woman deposited their tanks on one. I followed suit more clumsily, my head suddenly a thousand pounds lighter. I placed the headcloth next to the tank, grateful I'd been able to wrest the tank away from the older woman.

Then I bowed extravagantly to Melati, who clapped her hands and laughed. Then her smile fell, and she winced slightly—the motion must have disturbed her back. A male voice called out behind, and I turned to see Wayan hurrying down the stairs toward us, concern narrowing his brown eyes.

He called out in Indonesian, and the three women sobered. His mother's face grew stony, and Diah strode across the sand, obviously placating him. As she explained the situation, his eyes widened, then he crossed to place a gentle hand on his mother's upper arm.

As they conversed, Melati scoffed and patted his hand, then gestured to me and pointed to the tank. Wayan slid his eyes to mine, arching a brow. "You wanted to carry the tank? On your head?"

"I did, and your mother was kind enough to let me."

Melati resumed her conversation with Wayan, her voice commanding and assured. Then Diah joined in, obviously agreeing with the older woman and providing a united front.

Wayan shrugged and nodded.

Melati turned to me formally and pressed her hands together. But she only bowed her head, keeping her back straight. "Terima kasi."

The proper response flew into my mind. "Sama sama."

That made her cackle again, and she turned, moving in short steps across the sand toward the stairs.

Wayan scratched his head and turned back to me. "My mother said that since the tanks are here, she will return to our home and get the children ready for school. Which was her way of saying she would take today off and rest."

Diah turned to me, relief washing over her face. "Thank you for helping. Melati is hurting, but she is... proud."

"I was sitting outside and saw the three of you walk by. She was obviously in pain, and I wanted to help. It was the least I could do. One of you has carried my tank all week."

Wayan turned a worried frown from his mother to me,

then made an obvious effort to wipe it from his face. "I thank you also. My mother was one of the first porters in Tulamben and takes great pride in her job. But she grows older, and the work takes its toll."

Now I was feeling uncomfortable. I only wanted to lighten Melati's load a little. "Don't thank me. I was happy to help."

Wayan picked up on my discomfort and changed the subject, thank God. "I know you and Dawn aren't diving this morning. But you are diving tomorrow, yes?"

My mind went completely blank.

I stared at him for a long moment before remembering the schedule Dawn and I had planned. I bit back a confused laugh—*hell if I know!*—then nodded at him. "We look forward to it."

Wayan smiled. "So do I. So do *we*," he said with a head tip to Diah, who smiled.

I nodded, now feeling like it was time to make my exit. "We'll see you tomorrow, then."

And with that, I turned around and started toward the stairs, my heart a little lighter. My gaze traveled to the top of the stairs.

Dawn stood there, staring straight at me.

Chapter Seventeen

Dawn

WHEN I CAME out of the bungalow and crossed to the gazebo, I didn't find what I had expected. Cole was leaping over the pond and onto the path. Then he moved down it with purpose. Stumbling to a halt, I tried to figure out what was going on. He performed a pantomime with three women porters, including Wayan's wife and mother. The gestures and soft conversation ended with him taking Melati's tank and placing it on his head. A smile lifted my lips as I realized what he was doing.

Oh, Cole. Could you be any sweeter?

As they moved down the path, I followed. Though I went out our main door in the courtyard—the lotus pond was too big for me to jump.

Melati walked next to Cole, her arm looped around his elbow. She moved stiffly, occasionally moving a hand to rub her lower back, and I marveled at his ingenuity. I had no idea what he'd said to get her to relinquish her tank, but he'd done it without insulting her. In fact, all three women were smiling and obviously delighted with him.

Warmth radiated through my chest as I watched him, a mixture of pain at where we were and longing for where I wanted us to be. We needed to get everything out in the open. All of it. How he felt about me and vice versa. Then that fear stabbed through me again. Even if he did care enough to want me, would that be enough? Would I be enough?

I held back once they reached the resort pool, and soon Wayan trotted across the deck. He didn't see me and followed the women and Cole. I stayed put, not wanting to interrupt. But curiosity eventually got the better of me and I padded over the flagstone pool deck. I approached the landing as Melati reached the top step. Her face was haggard, pain etched in its many lines, and my heart clenched. Then she saw me, and the expression fled. As she passed, she smiled and nodded, but I wasn't fooled. Her movements were slow and stiff.

I turned to the beach below the stairs. Wayan and Diah stood in a circle with Cole, and the relief and gratitude on their faces were palpable. As was Cole's discomfort with being praised. Smiling, he took a big step backward as both gave him a pressed-hands bow, then turned and walked over the sand.

My heart pounded when he lifted his head and saw me.

His quiet smile transformed into an expression of wide-eyed shock that he quickly covered as he climbed the steps. His eyes held curiosity when he stopped two steps below me. We were nearly eye to eye.

"I didn't expect to find you here," he said.

"I came out to talk to you and saw you with the women. I followed. Melati looked like she wasn't feeling too good."

"She hurt her back, so I lent her a hand."

His usual self-effacing nature made me shake my head, a smile playing at my lips. "You're a good man, Cole Foster."

Laughing quietly, he stepped around me and tipped his head for me to join him. We walked together along the cement path, and my insides squirmed as I worked up the courage to say something about why I'd gone after him.

"I'm glad you came to find me," he said softly, both hands in his pockets. "I was waiting for you to wake up when the women walked by. I have something I need to say to you."

As we walked next to the big, rectangular pool, I swallowed hard, praying he wasn't about to say that I was too big of a risk for him. Fear twisted hard in my gut, and I let him go first. "What's that?"

He studied the still surface of the pool, and his smile returned. "It's fitting that we're walking by a pool right now. Last night, I thought a lot about the Olympics."

I didn't know what I had been expecting, but it wasn't that. "What brought that about?"

"That finals race was the most transformative moment of my life."

I relaxed slightly at the memory. "It certainly was. All that hard work and those early mornings finally paid off."

"Yeah, but it was a lot more than that. The hours before that race were a good part of why I won that gold medal. I damn near came unglued beforehand. I've never been so nervous."

I laughed, remembering the day vividly. Watching the race live. "I know! I was the one trying to calm you down, remember?"

He shot me a crooked smile, and my thudding heart slowed. Maybe he wasn't going to announce he never wanted to see me again. I wasn't sure why this was the subject he wanted to discuss now, but it was one of my favorite memories too. "Then it was time for your race, and you came out on the pool deck. You were so calm and focused, Cole! A man on a mission. Just looking at you sent a shiver through me." I didn't mention the shivers of an entirely different sort caused by my many rewatches of that video.

We passed the end of the pool and continued on the path toward our bungalow. He turned his head to glance at me. "That was because of you."

I smiled up at him. "So, all my *Go get 'em, tiger* texts actually made a difference?"

Cole didn't smile back. He watched me intently. My smile faded at the throbbing artery in his temple. His shoulders were tight and held rigidly.

"One text in particular," he murmured. "That one made all the difference."

I drew my brows together, racking my brain, but I couldn't remember specifically what I'd said. I couldn't remember saying anything profound.

We reached the door to our courtyard, and I pushed through it. I hadn't bothered to lock it when I went after him. Cole entered behind me and shut the door quietly. Placing his hand on my lower back, he guided me toward the table. "Have a seat. This is what I wanted to tell you."

As I sat adjacent to him, my mouth was suddenly parched. My heart took off again at the serious look on his face. He placed his hands on the table and flicked his thumbs. The artery still pulsed in his temple.

His nervousness did nothing to calm mine.

"It was the last text you sent. Right after I told you I needed to sign off and get ready."

"Good luck? Pretty sure I didn't say break a leg."

That brought a smile to his face, but it was gone as soon as it appeared. He met my eyes. "It was *I love you*." He shrugged, and the movement was uncomfortable, like he was trying to shake off his unease. "Look, I knew what you meant. You were sending the greatest wish you could to your best friend."

Even though Cole and I had been friends practically forever, we were conscious of the unacknowledged fact that we were of the opposite sex. And those three words were about as loaded as you could get. So, we avoided them. I knew he loved me as a friend, and likewise. In fact, now that I thought about it, I didn't remember Cole ever saying those words to me. But he had been heading to the greatest test of his life, and saying that had been appropriate, I'd thought.

Before I could say anything, he continued, still eyeing me steadily. "I knew what you intended, but I couldn't look away from my phone. I needed something to ground me, to calm my racing heart and nerves. A lot of race prep is mental work—visualization. So, I applied some mind exercises to your text. What if your words hadn't been a simple wish to a friend? What if you really did love me? As a man? I closed my eyes and visualized what that would look like. What that would *feel* like."

I couldn't have spoken now if my life depended on it. I was riveted to his words, though I had no idea any of this had happened. He took a deep breath, then slowly let it out. "This incredible sense of steady purpose washed over me. I put my mind to the race and what I was going to accomplish —nothing less than first place. I was going to go out there and push harder than I ever had. Because you loved me."

I smiled, my eyes filling with tears. "And you did. That's beautiful, Cole."

He shook his head rapidly. "You don't understand. Yet. The reason that text meant so much to me... why it meant everything to me"—his eyes held me captive and the naked, raw honesty in them floored me—"was because I was finally getting back what I'd felt for so long. Dawn, I love you. And I'm not talking about friendship. I've been in love with you for so long that I don't even know when it started. When we made love the other night, the final piece of the puzzle fell into place. And yet, you're the only one who has said those three words—even if you didn't mean them the same way I do. I need you to understand how I feel."

I was lightheaded, and there was a buzzing in my ears. Wasn't this why I went to find him in the first place? I drew a breath to speak, not knowing what would come out.

Cole leaned forward and placed his fingers softly against my lips. "Don't say anything. Not yet. Just by looking at you, I can tell this is a lot to take in. Give it a little time. But I need to know where we go from here, Dawn. I want a future with you, more than anything in the world. But you've got to believe in yourself first, and I think I can help with that. Because of you, I reached the greatest heights I could imagine. I want to do the same for you, but you've got to be on board. With us." He pushed to his feet. "I need to go for a swim. Think over what I said, and we'll talk after I get back. All right?"

I blinked and opened my mouth to answer, but nothing came out. I felt like a rag doll, with no bones.

Cole's been in love with me for years?

I cleared my throat and tried again. "Okay."

He rose and entered our bungalow. I sat there, numb and whirling, hardly able to move. A few minutes later, he came back out, dressed in swim trunks and freshly shaved. That he'd shaved told me he was going for a serious swim—

stubble rubbed his shoulders raw when he turned to breathe. "I'll be back in an hour or two."

I was frozen in my seat, equally blissful and terrified at his declaration. And so very afraid of saying the wrong thing. My answer needed to be unequivocal, and right now I could barely speak.

Which was why he wanted to give me time. "Thank you, Cole."

We stared at each other. He opened his mouth again, then shut it firmly. With a nod, he marched across the courtyard and left. He gently closed the door behind him, leaving me by myself.

TALL, shady trees bursting with leaves soared over our courtyard. Birds flitted between them, bringing the morning alive with birdsong. I lifted my head to a small yellow bird, yet hardly saw it, let alone heard it.

Cole loves me! He has for years!

That knowledge rocked me to my core, and a small flower bud buried deep in my heart began to unfurl. Not because someone was in love with me. *Cole* was in love with me.

The man who could have anyone.

And he wanted me. If he didn't think I was broken and beyond saving, why should I?

Except there was one very big subject still undetermined.

"He said he wanted a future with me," I whispered to the empty courtyard. Blake and I had been married at twenty. Much too young, I realized now. I had been so sure we were on the same page regarding our future together.

But I'd been terribly wrong.

I stood and walked toward the bungalow on numb feet. Opening the glass door, I was met with a blast of cold air. Surprised at the heat outside, I looked at the clock. It was after 9:00 a.m., later than I thought.

Kicking off my sandals, I paced across the marble floor. The tiles were smooth and cool under my feet as I tried to make sense of what I'd learned. How I felt about it.

And what I meant to do about it.

On the coffee table, my phone rang. I marched over and picked it up, hardly noticing the Unknown Number. "Hello?"

There was a hesitation, then, "Hi, Dawn."

I sagged into an armchair, all the strength leaving my legs. "*Blake?*"

His nervous laugh sounded through the phone, and I resisted the urge to wipe my hand on my shorts. "Don't sound so surprised. You had to know it was me from the Caller ID."

Anger welled in my stomach, a hot, orange furnace being stoked into life. "No, I didn't know it was you. Because I wiped every trace of you off my phone."

"Really?" He had the gall to sound hurt!

"What do you want?"

"I've been thinking about you lately. I wanted to hear your voice... though I was hoping for a warmer reception."

I raised a hand to my brow, trying to make sense of this call. "Why were you thinking about me? We're done, Blake."

"I know, but that doesn't mean I don't have regrets. Sometimes I wonder if we gave up too soon."

I vaulted to my feet and resumed pacing, much faster than before. "Too soon? I did everything possible to save our marriage! You weren't interested, remember?" Sunlight glinting on our pool caught my eye, golden confetti sparkling across the surface. "Do you even know I'm in Bali?"

"Bali?" He barked a laugh. "Why the hell would you be in Bali?"

That brought me to a complete stop. "How could you not know—after one year of dating and four years of marriage—that Bali is the place I've always dreamed of visiting?"

"You talked about a lot of places." His tone hardened, becoming defensive. More like the Blake I left. "How was I supposed to keep them all straight?"

"I did not talk about a lot of—why am I wasting my time with this?" I asked the room at large.

"Are you there by yourself?"

I started pacing again, now protective and wary. "Not that it's any of your damn business, but I'm here with a friend."

Blake laughed, a bitter, angry sound like nails going down a chalkboard. "I knew it! You're with Cole, aren't you? I knew there was more than *friendship* going on with you two!" The sneer in his voice when he said *friendship* made my lip curl.

"God, Blake. That's one of the saddest things about our marriage. Cole and I *were* only friends. Before we met and for our entire marriage. There was never anything romantic between us!"

Though that's not exactly true, is it? Cole had romantic feelings. But he's too good of a man to act on them when I was married. Instead, he distanced himself.

The realization made me even more angry.

Blake scoffed. "Sure. I'm supposed to believe that? That you didn't have the hots for Golden Boy?"

"I didn't, and that's my loss. I fell in love with you instead. But my eyes are wide-open now. To what you are and what Cole is. He has always been there when I needed him. And I'd do anything for him too. That's something you can't even comprehend because you are the most selfish, egotistical asshole on the planet."

"Forget I called. Sounds like I'm lucky we're over."

I stopped, and my eyes fell on the bed, still unmade. Images of the night Cole and I spent in it flashed through my mind. "Wrong again, Blake. I'm the lucky one. It took me going through hell to realize I love Cole, but at least it's not too late. So maybe I should thank you. If you hadn't been such an unbearable dick, he and I might not be here right now. And I wouldn't have the chance to tell him how much I love him and how lucky I am. So go to hell!"

"Can you even hear yourself right now? You're raving!"

A smile lit my face. "Not even close. I'm finally seeing clearly. I deleted you from my life for a reason, so don't ever call me again. You don't deserve me, you son of a bitch." I ended the call and tossed my phone on the coffee table.

Then I tipped my head back and let out a shout of pure joy to the heavens. Even before Cole told me he loved me, I'd been ready for a relationship with him. How ironic that it took a phone call from my idiot ex-husband to make me realize I loved him every bit as much as he loved me.

Why have I been so blind about this?

Closing my eyes, I pulled myself down to earth again. "I need to do something for Cole. Something special. I've been a drag this whole trip—it's the least I can do."

We had a lot to discuss, especially what *the future* meant.

My eye fell on the desk near the front door. A small souvenir bag of luwak coffee Cole had bought sat on top.

The sight of it brought me stumbling to a stop. A smile rose on my face as certainty filled me. I knew exactly what to do. Squaring my shoulders, I grabbed a bikini and changed, then tossed on a cover-up. Putting on flip-flops, I ran out of the bungalow, going the long way to my destination. I didn't want Cole to see me and ruin my surprise.

Besides, he'd see me soon enough.

Chapter Eighteen

Cole

DETERMINED to burn off my nervous, agitated energy, I attacked my swim workout, moving through all my strokes. I was currently on my tenth butterfly lap, and the soreness had left my body long ago. Now fatigue was setting in, and it was time to wind down. Reaching the deep end, I did a flip turn and cruised underwater, letting my body glide and my heart rate slow. When I touched the wall on the opposite side, I stood. Still breathing deeply, at least I wasn't damn near hyperventilating like I had been ten minutes ago.

The pool area was deserted. Since many bungalows had private pools, the big pool didn't get much use. Which suited me fine.

Sooner or later, I'd have to go back to the bungalow and face Dawn.

Face my fate.

After I'd told her how I felt about her, I hadn't expected

her to jump into my arms with declarations of love. Though that would have been nice.

But I had done it. Finally got the words out.

And she hadn't run away or immediately shot me down either, so maybe there was hope. I turned toward the far end of the pool and our bungalow beyond. Shock made me freeze. For the second time that day, Dawn appeared like a beautiful apparition.

She stood on the deck at the deep end, dressed in a loose cover-up. I ripped my goggles off and tossed them on the ground behind me. In one long motion, Dawn pulled off her cover-up, revealing a dark-red bikini, showing nearly all of her round, smooth, delicious body.

My breath caught.

My heart pounded.

She was so perfect.

I wanted her so badly.

But why was she here? To let me down easily?

Dawn entered the pool in a graceful dive, slicing through the water. I was transfixed, unable to move. She surfaced and swam toward me using a flowing, lithe freestyle stroke. Ten feet away, she rose and stood on her feet. Beads of water slid down her toned torso, meeting the pool surface at her waist. Her full breasts peeked from the triangle of red fabric covering them, reminding me of what lay underneath.

Catching my gaze, she stepped toward me. Her eyes were confident, powerful, and I was completely under her spell. Whether the news was good or not.

Dawn was completely silent as she strode toward me.

I ached to touch her, yet was afraid to move. Only my heart moved, racing frantically in my chest.

Stopping before me, Dawn gently cupped my face in

both hands and lowered my head. She tilted hers and pressed her full, warm lips to mine. Lightning raced through my body at the contact, hope at what it might mean.

Yet I still remained motionless. Needing confirmation.

Sliding one hand behind my head, she increased the pressure, probing her tongue into my mouth. She closed her fist, grabbing a handful of my hair as her mouth devoured mine. This was no tentative, questioning kiss.

She was answering my question.

I met her tongue with mine. Our kiss was wet, long, and incredibly hot. If anything, my pulse pounded even faster.

Finally, she pulled back. I opened my eyes, and her face was inches from mine. She stared at me, a tiny smile raising her lips. "I love you too, Cole."

My relief was so great my knees almost buckled. I flung my arms around her, pulling her tight against me. Tears sprang to my eyes. I'd dreamed of this moment for so long, I never wanted to let her go.

"I'm sorry it took me so long to figure it out."

I placed a knuckle under her chin and tilted her face up. "None of that matters. We're here right now. Together."

She nodded and danced her fingers over my pecs, then slid her eyes to the restaurant, done with breakfast but soon setting up for lunch. "We have a lot to talk about. One subject in particular, and I'd rather not discuss it in public. Are you done with your swim?"

I jerked a nod, still hardly able to form words as we climbed out and redressed. I could have been filled with helium. I was buoyant, ready to fly away at any moment. As we strolled back to our room, our hands laced together. I couldn't have said if she took my hand or I took hers—it just happened naturally.

Like it was meant to be.

After we entered our courtyard, we took our seats at the outdoor table once more. I gave her a smile. "Is this becoming our *serious talk* table?"

She smiled back, but it was shaky. "I hope not, but we have one more thing we need to discuss, okay?"

"Of course. Nothing is off-limits." I leaned forward and took her hand. That seemed to steady her.

She inhaled a deep, long breath, then let it out in a rush. "You mentioned wanting a future with me. But I need to know what that looks like, Cole. What your vision of the future is. It might seem silly to talk about this when we haven't even become a couple yet, but it's important. I might not be able to have children."

I swallowed hard but kept my face encouraging. This was her central fear—the one thing that was holding her back. I couldn't blow it now. "I'd love to have a family. Two, three kids. And yeah, I can see them with you." I tightened my hold on her hand. "If that's not meant to be, we can look into adoption. And if *that* doesn't work out, we'll still have each other. I want you, Dawn."

"Are you sure you really mean that?"

"More than sure. With or without children, you're perfect for me. You were right about us being each other's mirror. I wish to God you could see yourself the way I do."

She smiled again, and this time it was more certain. "When we get back, I'm going to make an appointment with a fertility specialist. That way we'll know... if I'm the problem."

I leaned closer and clasped her face between my hands. Needing her to understand my next words. "Listen to me. If you need to do that for your own peace of mind, I'll stand behind you one hundred percent. But I love you exactly as you are right now. You're an incredible teacher and your kids all love you. Seeing a doctor isn't going to change that. Neither is having children. If we're meant to have kids, we will. You are exactly enough. Right now." I stopped for a moment to emphasize my next words.

"Dawn. I. Choose. You."

Her face crumpled and she flew into my lap. Great, wracking sobs tore from her throat as she wrapped both arms around me. Her entire body convulsed with her release. I cradled her body close, enveloping her in my arms, and kissed her damp hair. Then I rested my lips against the strands and closed my eyes. "Let it out, baby. You've been holding this inside for much too long. I'll keep you safe. I promise."

I let her cry against my chest, moving her legs next to my hip so she sat sideways on my lap. I held her and stroked her back, then her hair, then her back again, until she was finally cried out.

"Better?" I asked softly.

"You have no idea how much."

Her body became heavier in my arms as she relaxed. Then she opened her mouth in an enormous yawn, making me smile. "Did you get much sleep last night?"

"No," she murmured against me. "Did you?"

"Very little."

She lifted her head to stare into my eyes. "Do you want to take a nap with me?"

"That is the best idea you've had all day." I wasn't lying. I was practically sleepwalking at this point. After the restless night, the stress of telling her I loved her, the brutal swim workout, then this catharsis, I could probably fall asleep right here.

She nodded and rose to her feet, pushing gently against my chest for support. I hung the Do Not Disturb sign on the courtyard door, then we entered the bungalow and closed the curtains. She changed back into her white tank top and shorts while I put on a clean pair of underwear. Then we slid into the bed together.

I curled behind her, loosely holding her shoulder with one bent arm as I shimmied my knees behind her. A blissful sigh eased from me. "You have no idea how long I've wanted to do this. Just lie here holding you like this."

She started shaking, and I lifted my head, not understanding. She couldn't remain quiet any longer, laughing out loud. "You *have* done this before. Three nights ago."

"What? I did not!"

She turned her head to grin at me. "Oh, yeah, you did. You were sound asleep. I woke up and we were like this— the day we went to Ubud. It was wonderful, but I knew you'd be rather embarrassed if you woke up. So I snuck out of bed and went outside."

I remembered that morning. I also remembered waking up hard as a rock. Maybe she didn't notice. "Huh. Really?"

"Yep. I also got a very good measure of what I've been missing all these years. Though that paled in comparison to the next night."

I groaned, heat flushing across my face as her giggles came back. I kissed her shoulder. "Well, don't be too disappointed if you don't get a repeat performance right now, okay? I'm barely awake."

"You could never disappoint me." She took my hand and brought it to her lips. "We've got time for a nice, long nap. I made a dinner reservation for us at six."

"Really?" I asked, already warm and woozy. "When did you do that?"

"Right before I came to the pool. But you'll have to wait to find out the specifics. It's a surprise."

"Mmm," I said, not really capable of pondering her surprise. Instead, I gathered her tighter against me and pulled her hair aside. With an easy sigh, I pressed my cheek to the back of her neck and fell asleep instantly.

Chapter Nineteen

Dawn

THE EASTERN HORIZON was dark as Cole and I walked toward the restaurant. Mt. Agung loomed to the west, a dark cone lit from behind by a pink-crimson sky, signaling the end of a momentous day. Neither of us was dressed up —I wore black capris with a lacy tank top and Cole was in gray cargo shorts and a button-up shirt.

We weren't going to a fancy dinner, after all. Nerves fluttered through my stomach, but I ignored them, determined to soldier on.

I inhaled a deep breath of the tropical air, recalling the feeling of being wrapped up with Cole that afternoon. Sleeping snuggled next to him—with both of us fully aware of the fact—was almost more intimate than sex. It had been heavenly. The best nap of my life.

I'd woken two hours later, refreshed and alone in bed. Across the room, Cole sat at the desk, eating a protein bar. Several empty wrappers lay next to him, reminding me neither of us had eaten breakfast. Or lunch. Not a huge issue for me, but I had no doubt Cole had worked up an appetite.

We spent the afternoon lazing by our private pool, both of us getting used to our new status. Other than a few kisses, we refrained from overt advances. We had all night to discover each other.

Again.

Hands clasped, we crossed the pool deck and stepped into the airy restaurant. Over the week, we'd gravitated to the same table. Set for two, it sat at the edge of the restaurant overlooking the pool and beach. Kirana had become our regular server, and she was who I had spoken to that morning. Seeing us coming now, she floated to our table, elegant and beautiful in a long eggplant-colored skirt and a tunic of subtle sage-green-and-white pattern. She held out a chair for me.

Smiling, she looked at us both. "One small Bintang and one large tonight?"

I shook my head. "Make it two large ones." I was going to need extra fortification tonight, a little Dutch courage.

She brought our two beers right away and inclined her head. "Your first course will be ready shortly."

After she left, Cole placed his napkin in his lap and gave me a puzzled smile. "I don't even get to choose what I'm eating? You're bossing me around already?"

I laughed and took a swig of beer. "Hardly. It's a fixed menu, that's all."

"Dawn Hammond, woman of mystery."

"Maybe you don't know everything about me after all."

A small thrill raced through me as he reached across the table and took my hand. "I'm sure I don't. But I mean to find out."

A band was playing soft, romantic music and several

couples were dancing. I enjoyed dancing, but tonight wasn't the night for cutting a rug. But the music provided a lovely backdrop to the warm evening.

Kirana appeared, carrying a platter in one hand and a row of dipping sauces in the other. She placed them between us, and my stomach clenched at the recognizable shapes on the large plate. "Your first course tonight is *belalang goreng*, fried grasshoppers. Many Balinese eat this as a snack. The sauces are peanut, spicy sambal, and sweet chili. Enjoy."

As she floated away, Cole burst into laughter, his eyes round. "You're kidding me! You ordered the exotic meal? *You?*"

I couldn't help smiling even as the thought of eating a grasshopper sent an oily twist through my stomach. "Yes. Me. I've put you through hell the last couple of days, Cole. You did everything possible to support me. All I did was take—I pulled into my shell like a turtle. And this morning you risked it all. For us. I wanted to do something special for you."

His eyes softened, though the smile remained. "You didn't have to do this, though I'm really looking forward to it. And sometimes going for the gold pays off, doesn't it?" He winked and picked up a grasshopper. Studying the sauces, he dipped it in the peanut sauce, tipped his head back, and dropped it into his open mouth. Across the table, I could hear the crunch and swallowed hard.

Cole swallowed and smacked his lips. "They're really good! A little spicy—they dusted them with something. You've only eaten a protein bar all day. You gonna try one?" His grin widened.

"Absolutely. If grasshoppers get your seal of approval, I don't need more." Ignoring my flip-flopping stomach, I picked one up by a single leg and dunked it in the sweet chili sauce. The leg broke off as I pulled it out, and I had to grasp it by the body. I was unable to repress a shudder as I rushed it to my mouth, downed a huge swig of Bintang, chewed frantically, and swallowed.

Brows halfway up his forehead, Cole sat motionless across the table and waited for my reaction.

Surprisingly, my stomach accepted the insect with hardly a qualm. "Okay. That one went down without protest. With the chili sauce, it wasn't too bad."

Cole spooned several grasshoppers onto his plate and descended with glee, trying each of the sauces. I ate more carefully, avoiding the spicy one.

We had eaten most of the grasshopper extravaganza when Kirana returned. She moved the belalang goreng to an empty table, then set down three steaming dishes. She pointed to the first one, which looked like reddish-colored fried rice.

Fried rice! I can eat that! My confidence grew.

Kirana indicated the dish. "*Lawar merah.* Our version is made with cabbage, water chestnuts, chicken, and rice. Our chef uses a special mixture of spices mixed with what gives the dish its distinctive color. Chicken blood. *Merah* is red in Indonesian."

My stomach clenched at her last sentence, the grasshoppers now not so happy in my stomach. But the next dish looked like large gnocchi in a brown broth, and the potato pasta looked very appetizing by comparison.

I smiled as Kirana pointed to that dish next. "And this is *ancruk,* sago worms cooked in a thin broth."

Cole watched me closely as the smile fell from my face.

Okay, not gnocchi. I can still do this.

I nodded firmly at him and examined the final dish,

which looked like pork rinds, loose in a serving bowl. "And what is this wonderful delicacy?"

"*Keripik ceker*," Kirana replied. "Chicken feet chips. They provide a little crunch to contrast the other two dishes." With a bright smile, she nodded to us then glided back toward the kitchen.

I took a deep breath and stared at the three dishes.

"You can order something else, you know," Cole said softly. "I don't want you to be miserable."

"Nonsense. This is why a person travels. To try new things. Let's dig in." Besides, this meal was the one thing Cole wanted to experience the most since we landed on the island. I refused to let him down.

Cole scooped a big spoonful of the blood stuff on his plate while I used a slotted spoon to place three worms on mine. Then, trying to project more confidence than I felt, I loaded up my plate with the other two entrees.

I wish I could say these dishes went down as well as the grasshoppers had, but that wasn't the case. I managed to swallow the first worm without chewing but took more time with the second. It was thick and rubbery, making my throat clench as I swallowed. I chased it quickly with a liberal amount of Bintang.

Taking a forkful of the lawar merah, I prepared myself. But as I chewed the chicken and rice dish, I hadn't prepared myself fully for the thick, coppery taste coating every bite. I gagged, then swallowed a giant drink of Bintang to cover it. Fortunately, the chips were easier to eat and actually tasty when dipped in the sauces. I nibbled around the bones, trying not to think about them being feet.

Meanwhile, Cole dug into the dinner like a man eating his last supper. "The lawar is kind of weird but not bad. And the worms have absorbed the flavor of the broth really well." He picked up a chicken-foot chip and tore into it with a smile. After swallowing, he cocked his head, considering. "The chicken feet are similar to wings, actually. Only crispier."

Wings. Pretend I'm eating wings!

I ate another but couldn't convince myself, then switched to a worm, quickly followed by a beer chaser. I finished my Bintang before Cole was even half finished with his, and Kirana quickly brought me a second. I found that a bite of lawar, immediately followed by a drink of Bintang, worked okay. Though my stomach was definitely not enjoying itself now.

I needed conversation to distract myself. "I've never seen a food you won't eat. How do you do that? You like everything that your mouth comes in contact with?"

Cole raised his eyes sharply at that last sentence, a seductive smile rising. "Some things more than others."

I grinned back. My comment hadn't been intentional, but it worked to distract me from my misery.

Cole took a drink of beer. "Eating whatever's put in front of me was a natural byproduct of swim workouts. When I was training for the Olympics, I ate five to seven thousand calories a day just to keep from losing weight. Food became another part of the workout—whether I enjoyed the meal or not didn't matter. And sometimes our chefs got creative to get calories into us. I learned to deal with it. This meal tastes pretty good to me, though I'm not sure I'd order the lawar again."

My stomach took a long roll at the thought.

Another distraction—pronto! "Can I ask you something?"

Cole tilted his head, watching me evenly. "You can ask me anything. I've got no secrets from you."

"After the Olympics, you went back to Austin. You got together with Angie not too long after. How come you didn't ask her to move with you when you came back home?"

"It wasn't that kind of relationship." His voice was tight, and there was an undercurrent to his words.

"What kind of relationship?"

"The kind where I wanted her to move halfway across the country to stay together."

"Because of me?"

He shifted in his seat and sighed. "At the time, I would have answered no to that question. But looking back on it now, I'm sure your being newly single played a part. I was part of a couple, but when I compared you and Angie, there *was* no comparison. I couldn't see a place for her in my life in San Bernadino. So we called it quits."

"We?" That was the undercurrent I was picking up.

"Me. Our breakup was pretty ugly. We were in a steady relationship, but it was because I was in a set routine. She became a part of that. When I got the chance to take over the gym from Coach Terry and have you in my life again, I didn't hesitate. Angie didn't expect the breakup and was pretty upset."

"Do you keep in touch?"

He shook his head. "We made a clean break. Better for both of us that way."

"Neither of us has had the best luck with love, have we?"

Cole raised his eyes to mine, holding them steady. "Maybe because we were with the wrong people."

"That's what I believe. I regret it took so long for me to figure it out."

Cole shot me a lopsided smile. "Not so long. We're only in our mid-twenties."

I was only married to Blake for four years, though at times it had felt like forty. But Cole was right. We had plenty of time to figure out the future—whatever it would hold for us.

We went back to our meal and my beer steadily declined. A third giant beer was out of the question—I was already rather buzzed. But the Bintang did help the food go down without me gagging.

Not too much, anyway.

Cole swallowed another worm. "You never did say, was there anything specific that cemented your feelings about us this morning? That was quite an attitude shift. You looked really shell-shocked when I left, but when you joined me in the pool, I've never seen you more confident."

I sat up in my chair, then placed a hand over my stomach as it protested at the quick movement. "With everything that happened, I never told you, did I? I got a phone call after you left. From Blake, of all people."

A wall flew over Cole's face as he hid his reaction. That alone told me he had strong feelings about Blake.

"He gave me some bullshit about getting divorced too soon. Then he blew up that I was in Bali with you. I let him have it. That you were the one who was always there for me, not him. I started telling him all the things I love about you, then wondered why I never voiced them before. Even to myself. It was so obvious! I ended by telling him to never contact me again. That he didn't deserve me."

A slow smile raised Cole's lips. This one wasn't seductive. It was euphoric. "One hundred percent true. What did he say to that?"

"He didn't. I hung up on him and came here to make

the dinner reservation. Then I went to the pool to tell you I love you."

He took my hand, interlacing his fingers through mine. "I love you too."

His plate was empty, and I didn't think my stomach would accept any more bugs, blood, or feet.

"You want to see what's on offer for dessert?" he asked.

I shook my head, the movement sending another greasy roil through my stomach. "I don't think I could take it."

He grinned and squeezed my hand. "Thanks for doing this. I loved it, even if I feel guilty that you didn't."

"Don't feel guilty. You deserve it." I took a sip of water. I was at the point where more beer would be a very bad idea. Saliva flooded my mouth as my belly made another rolling lurch. "We'd better head out, and you might have to help me back to the bungalow. I really think I might throw up."

Chapter Twenty

Cole

I WATCHED Dawn closely as we walked back to our bungalow, draping an arm around her shoulders. She kept both arms wrapped over her stomach and took a deep, long breath.

"Are you okay?"

"I'm pretty nauseated. Maybe that second beer wasn't such a good idea."

When we entered the room, she stepped into the soft glow of the nightstand lights, and what I had feared on the short journey from the restaurant was revealed. Her face had a distinct greenish tint to it. "I think you better crawl straight into bed and go to sleep."

She stopped and wrinkled her nose, her jaw moving back and forth. "I need to brush my teeth first. God, I need to brush my teeth."

As she trudged to the bathroom, I undressed, pulling on a pair of loose workout shorts. When she came back out, I helped her into bed and drew the covers up over her, then kissed her forehead. It was slightly damp with sweat, making me frown.

She saw it and gave my hand a brief squeeze. "Don't worry, I'll live."

"I certainly hope so. I'll be right next to you if you need anything, all right?" With a final stroke of my finger down her cheek, I rose and went into the bathroom. Even after nearly a week, I still wasn't used to the blast of warm air I encountered upon entering the outdoor room. Fortunately, the tall walls made it completely private. I had to admit brushing my teeth after that meal was a pretty wonderful feeling.

I'd enjoyed the exotic meal, except for Dawn's obvious misery. Still, I couldn't see myself ordering grasshoppers or worms again anytime soon.

When I climbed into bed, Dawn was already asleep. A vertical line remained between her brows. After our momentous day, I longed to snuggle tight but didn't want to disturb her. With a sigh, I settled on my back and was surprised when my eyelids grew heavy immediately.

When I awoke sometime later, I was instantly aware something was off. A glance at the nightstand clock told me it was just after midnight, so I'd been asleep for several hours—we'd turned in early. The door to the bathroom was ajar and a sliver of light pierced our cocooned bed. I glanced over at Dawn's side of the bed.

Empty.

That's what woke me.

The sound of retching brought me to my feet, and I hurried to the bathroom door. Pushing it open, I ducked my head inside. Dawn was on her knees in front of the toilet, both hands pressed against the side of her face.

"I take it dinner isn't settling any better."

She turned a pair of bleary eyes to me, then leaned forward and gripped the sides of the toilet. The sound of her vomiting, followed by her low moan, made me wince. I crossed the tile floor and hunkered down next to her. With one hand, I gathered her hair and held it as she convulsed again. Eventually, she sat back on her heels and flushed the toilet. Her eyes were closed, and she breathed in deep pants.

"Are you doing better now, or do we need to get you to a doctor?"

She gave me a weak smile. "I need to get that food out of my body. Then I'll be okay." She had no sooner finished the sentence than she whipped her head back to the toilet and wretched again.

I held her hair and rubbed her back with my other hand, trying to at least provide a sympathetic presence. There wasn't much else I could do.

When she finished puking, she flushed but remained over the bowl. "You don't have to do this. Go back to bed, Cole."

I tucked a lock of black hair behind her ear. "I know I don't have to. We're still friends, you know. This is something a friend would do. Your boyfriend Cole would probably run screaming." Actually, a fuzzy warmth was spreading through my entire body at being able to do this for her. This was exactly the kind of thing a caring boyfriend would do.

She laughed before flinching, gripping her belly with one hand. "My abs hurt. I know there was nothing wrong with the food because you're fit as a fiddle."

"I still might barf out of sympathy, but the bugs and blood didn't upset my stomach."

"Oh God!" Apparently, that was the wrong thing to say as she started another round of heaving.

When she was done, I regripped her hair and massaged her shoulder with my free hand. "Are you sure you're okay?"

She nodded and flushed again. "I'm already feeling better."

We sat on the floor for several more minutes, both silent. I rubbed her back as she rested her head on my shoulder. I closed my eyes and kissed the top of her head, incredibly grateful to be comforting her.

Smiling faintly, she placed her hand over mine and squeezed. "How many times have you held someone's hair while they threw up?"

I thought for a moment. "Only once. We were at the world championships and afterward a bunch of us went to a bar. There was a *lot* of drinking. I did my fair share but was in better shape than most. One guy was so hammered, when he started throwing up, we were afraid he'd choke. So we dragged him into the bathroom. Two other guys held his arms, and I had the honor of holding his hair back. He was the only guy on the team with longish hair. Your hair is much nicer to hold."

Dawn started laughing halfway through my story and slumped onto her hip. "Scarecrow, you really know how to draw the short end of the stick."

"The other two guys might argue with that. At least I was out of the splash zone."

Laughing, she sat up straight. "I think it's all out now. I want to drink some water and brush my teeth, then I'll come back to bed."

I nodded and pushed upright. Grasping both of her hands in mine, I helped her to her feet, then left the room to give her some privacy. When she parted the mosquito net and climbed into bed, I pulled her against my chest. My heart was so full I could hardly breathe. She snuggled against me, one hand stroking my chest.

"We're supposed to dive tomorrow morning," I murmured. "You want me to cancel?"

"No. This is our last chance. I'll be fine by morning— mostly fine, anyway. I'm already much better." She kissed my chest softly, then settled against me again. "Thank you for pampering me in there."

I smiled and rested my cheek against her head. "It was nothing. I can't believe you went through that for me."

"I wanted to make you happy. Sorry I ended up such a mess."

I stroked the soft strands of her hair. "I can't tell you how happy you make me. And holding you in my arms like this is heaven, as far as I'm concerned."

She sighed. "I had big plans for another night full of mind-blowing sex. So much for that idea."

My chest shook with laughter. "We have plenty of time for that. Besides, I'm not sure a night full of sex is realistic after eating bugs, chicken feet, and drinking blood. I think you'd better stay with more normal foods, like the chicken sate."

"Can we not talk about food right now, Cole?"

That only made me laugh harder, even though I felt awful for her. I could feel her lips rise into a smile against my chest. "Consider the subject banished. Get some good sleep, and we'll make our last day in Bali the best one."

She made a soft hum in response but was already falling asleep in my arms. Adjusting my hold on her slightly, I closed my eyes with a contented sigh. Maybe this wasn't falling asleep after mind-blowing sex, but it was still the stuff my dreams were made of.

———

Dawn's guess was correct, and she was mostly recovered by morning. Her belly was still sore, but she pronounced herself perfectly fit to dive. I woke up with the kernel of an idea forming. By the time we went to breakfast, it was fully formed. I couldn't wait to set it in action, but I needed to get some privacy first. After we finished eating would be perfect.

I gazed down at my banana pancakes, bacon, and giant cheese omelet, then raised a brow at her two slices of dry toast. "You sure you don't want some of my breakfast?"

"No way. I'm not tempting fate. If the toast settles okay, I'll eat more for lunch. What do you want to do for our last dinner?"

I tried to look casual, like I was mulling over her question. "Probably not bugs."

She had been lifting her toast and froze to glare at me. "Definitely not bugs."

I grinned back and drank some coffee. "Let's dress up a little. I brought a pair of slacks and a nice shirt. Do you have a dress?"

"As a matter of fact, I do. A rather sexy black number."

I waggled my eyebrows at her. "I can't wait to see it."

"Good things come to those who wait." Her smile was sending the blood in my veins straight south, so I stared at the ocean for a distraction. "Sounds like you're looking forward to our last dives."

"I really am. It's my last chance to see that wild fish."

"Make sure you point it out if you see it."

Again, she described the fish she'd seen our first day diving. What she depicted hardly sounded real. "Don't worry, if it's there, you'll notice it."

I tore into my pancakes, still hungry after the turmoil of yesterday. Not to mention the lack of food. One meal of bugs and blood didn't make for a full stomach. Especially mine.

After we left and were walking by the dive shop, I stopped and turned to Dawn. "Why don't you go on ahead? I want to know how many people we're diving with this morning. I'm kind of hoping it will be only the two of us and Wayan. I'll catch up in a minute."

As she ambled down the path, I ducked in and confirmed that we were the only two guests diving. Which made me happy, but wasn't actually my goal. After peeking to make sure Dawn wasn't lingering, I hurried back to the restaurant and flagged down Kirana.

She was only too happy to help, and within a few minutes, I had everything set up. A grin split my face as I strolled back to get ready to dive.

If I had anything to say about it, our final day in Bali would be one to remember.

Chapter Twenty-One

Dawn

I PICKED up my two weight pouches, ready to head down the beach and toward the Liberty. Our final day in Bali looked to be a beautiful one, with hardly a breeze and bright sunshine warming my shoulders. The sea softly lapped against the black sand, which would make the entry wearing heavy scuba equipment much easier.

Cole straightened and shaded his eyes with his hand, then turned to Wayan. "I don't see the porters, and I was wondering about your mother. How is she doing?"

"Better. Our son is sick, so she is staying home to help with him." Wayan gave them a smile. "Which will also rest her back for a few days."

Cole nodded. "I'm glad to hear that. I hope she gets better soon."

Wayan broke into laughter. His teeth were vividly white, making for a sharp contrast against his rich brown skin. "I think she will miss you. She laughed all last night about you carrying that tank on your head. Thank you for your help."

"It was nothing."

I shook my head slightly and smiled. It was much more than nothing and Cole knew that. After breakfast, I had been changing into a swimsuit when Cole returned to the bungalow and delivered the good news that it would only be the two of us diving with Wayan. I was delighted, though we would miss Steph and Quinn, who had left for home.

Cole picked up his weight pouches. "Ready to head down the beach?"

"Yep. Let's go." I slipped into line behind Wayan, and a thrill tickled down my spine when Cole rested his hand against the small of my back. He'd never been shy about providing support when I needed it, but now his touch was different. For one thing, he softly brushed his thumb back and forth over my T-shirt. I turned my head and gave him a smile. He answered with a slow wink.

Several minutes after we reached the clearing, Diah appeared, accompanied by two women I didn't recognize. They deposited our scuba tanks on the picnic table before retreating to the shade near the tree line.

After kitting up, Cole and I followed Wayan down the beach. We entered the water and submerged. On each dive, the divemaster had led us into the ocean at slightly different points so our journey to the wreck was always different. I was amazed at how he recognized every square inch of underwater scenery.

The Liberty was an extremely popular dive site, but we had gotten an early start and were rewarded by being the only ones on the wreck. Golden sunbeams flickered over the superstructure. Massive schools of fish clustered in large balls before loosely unforming, only to mix together again. A school of sleek silver fish darted past us impossibly fast. I could hardly turn quickly enough to follow their motion. Then the group shifted as one and disappeared in a new direction. My pulse thrummed as a different school whizzed past us, their yellow tails blurry with speed. Cole and I exchanged grins.

It was magical.

We continued across the deck of the ship, and Wayan led us down passageways and up a staircase encrusted with coral. Large holes had been cut into the ship for closer exploration, but being new divers, we stayed on the outside of the mammoth structure.

Wayan swept his head in a broad movement, searching for animals. Then he froze, squinting into the blue. He darted his hand out, pointing frantically as he spun toward us. I followed his finger as a massive, odd fish swam by only twenty feet away. It was one of the strangest creatures I'd ever seen. Pale and luminous, it was shaped like a dinner plate held upright—thin and nearly circular in shape, except for two giant triangular fins protruding from the top and the bottom of the fish. Its body alone, without the fins, had to be at least five feet in diameter.

Wayan scribbled on a white waterproof slate. Bursts of bubbles exited his regulator, indicating how excited he was. With wide eyes, he turned the slate and showed us: mola mola. Sunfish!

I turned to Cole, who smiled around his regulator, his eyes full of wonder. We watched the giant fish glide past, barely moving its two fins to propel itself. I took Cole's hand, grateful to share such an experience with him, and he held back tightly.

We continued our tour with Wayan finding a stunning

moray eel. The nearly white creature was marked with black circular bands and dotted with yellow spots. Bright yellow eyes stared at us. Wayan indicated it was a snowflake moray.

And this fantastical world has existed down here the whole time, only we never knew it!

As we slowly finned back toward the shore, we passed a coral bommie—a rock formation twenty feet long covered in hard and soft corals. Colorful sea fans fought for space, and more tropical fish darted about. The scene was like an underwater city, with its inhabitants going about their daily business. I gasped as the shape I'd been looking for appeared.

My mystery fish!

Like before, this one was a solitary creature roughly a foot long. I grabbed Cole's arm and pointed toward the amazing animal. He stilled, his eyes growing wide as he stared at it. I still could hardly believe it was real. How did something like that exist?

Like the one I had observed previously, this specimen had a thin, oval-shaped body and a broad, fanlike tail. Its pattern was also divided. The top of the fish was black, and iridescent yellowish-orange streaks reflected the sunlight, appearing to shimmer. The lower half was pure black with an even pattern of large white spots. The fish carried a pair of Angelina Julie-like lips—bright orange and pursed in a perpetual kiss.

Wayan glanced and saw us transfixed by the unreal fish. Pulling out his slate, he wrote: clown triggerfish. Then he grinned at us and nodded, obviously enjoying our reaction.

I turned to Cole and clapped, excited he'd gotten to see the fish. He inclined his head in acknowledgment and we continued toward the shore. We swam side by side, and I noted how much more natural he looked in the water now. He no longer used his arms to balance himself and his air consumption had improved drastically over the week.

I couldn't help grinning to myself, a little delighted that I took to a sport involving water more easily than he had.

When we reached the shallows, all three of us stood. Wayan tucked his fins under one arm. "We still have one more dive on the drop-off near Haven, but I'm not sure we can beat that one."

"That was incredible!" Cole said. "That huge fish was called a mola mola?"

"Yes! They come through here sometimes, but it's still unusual to see one. We were lucky!"

"Even without the mola mola, it would have been an incredible dive," I said. "I saw a clown triggerfish the other day and wanted Cole to see it. I don't think he believed me when I described it!"

Cole burst into laughter. I loved the sound of it, pure and uninhibited. "You're right—I didn't."

We took off our tanks and withdrew the weight pouches once more before making the trek back to Haven. Cole and I relaxed on the stone seawall while the staff changed our gear to fresh tanks. Then we followed the women to the southern area where I had come across Cole yesterday morning.

We shared a private smile at the memory, then got in the water for our final dive. Wayan was right. We dove over a beautiful, sparkling reef vivid with life, but nothing could match the Liberty. Which was why it was one of the top dive attractions on the island, if not *the* top.

But we had no idea when we'd next be underwater, so I took the time to fully enjoy the experience, taking in the colors of the reef, the bright, almost fluorescent fish, and the other creatures that lived there.

And most especially, I was conscious of who I was diving with. And the fact that Cole's and my relationship was fundamentally different now. I swam up to him and took his hand, and we were joined as we drifted over the kaleidoscopic, thriving reef.

I wouldn't have it any other way.

WE SPENT the afternoon alternately packing and relaxing by our pool. I tossed a pair of shorts into my suitcase, noting there was more room since Cole had eaten all the snacks I'd brought along. I heaved a sigh. "I wish we had another week. I'm not ready to go home yet."

"Me neither. I could get used to this."

I lifted my head and our eyes met. He strolled toward me, still wearing damp swim trunks. Tucking two locks of hair behind my ears, he bent his head and kissed me. The sensation of our lips softly melding together was still new. And completely thrilling.

With a soft hum, I broke the kiss to smile at him. "I could definitely get used to this. You're right, though. This was an awful long way to travel for a one-week trip. We'll have to remember that for next time."

A playful smile tugged at his lips. "Next time, huh? Already planning it?"

"Not really, but it's fun to dream about. Steph told me she and Quinn live on a resort island off the coast of Florida. Might be fun to visit them sometime."

"Right. Sandpiper Cay."

"She said it's a pretty adult atmosphere and can get loud. I'm not sure that's our style."

He brushed his finger down the bridge of my nose. "We've only been together a day. We don't have a style yet."

I laughed. "Can't argue with that. But I'm going to look into that other place Steph mentioned. Half Moon Bay Resort on St. Croix."

He drew me against his chest. "Wherever you lead, I'll follow."

"And wherever you lead, I'll follow." I closed my eyes and slipped my arms around his waist as he wrapped me in a solid embrace. I held still, enjoying the sensation of being in his arms. At how different it was, yet still home to me. Always home to me.

Eventually, I propped my chin on his chest and looked at the clock. "It's after five. I'm going to take a shower and get ready for dinner. Our last dinner in Bali. Maybe we should splurge on a nice bottle of wine or champagne tonight?"

He smiled, and there was something mischievous in it. "That sounds like a great idea. I'll let you have the first shower, then I'll go."

I arched a brow. "We could shower together, you know."

"Mmm." He whisked his lips over mine. "You have no idea how tempting that is. But this is our last night. Let's draw things out a little."

"Ah—you're going to tease me. Is that it?"

"Tease. Taste. Tantalize." He punctuated each word with a kiss, and my core was becoming molten. Then he took a large, deliberate step back and grinned. "But not yet. Get in the shower."

I trailed a finger over his arm as I moved to the closet.

Draping my black dress over my arm, I headed toward the bathroom with a seductive stare. "All right. We'll do things your way. But I hope you're up to the challenge, Cole. Now you've set expectations."

He leaned back against the desk and crossed his legs at the ankles. With his short, light-brown hair and sharply defined jaw, he was incredibly handsome. Chiseled. "I'm always up to the challenge, baby."

Chapter Twenty-Two

Cole

I CHOSE my outfit for the night, a dressy shirt and slacks, and was laying them out on the bed when Dawn emerged from the bathroom sooner than I'd expected. She was dressed in only a towel, which was thoroughly distracting, and the black dress was folded over her arm.

"Changed my mind," she said, holding up a hair dryer and flat iron. "You don't get to see me until I'm all made up and ready to go. You can get ready in the bathroom, and I'll change in here."

As much as I wanted to rip that towel off her, letting my arousal build slowly throughout the evening had its own rewards. I inclined my head. "As you wish."

She laughed at the *Princess Bride* reference, and I headed in to shower and shave.

Half an hour later, I finger combed my hair and took one last look at my jaw in the mirror, making sure I hadn't missed any spots. I glanced at my watch and smiled. Five forty-five. We were right on time.

Moving to the bathroom door, anticipation built as I opened it. Both at seeing Dawn and for the night in general. Our first real night as a couple. Though last night had been incredibly endearing and made me love Dawn even more, it hadn't been terribly high on the romantic scale.

Tonight would be different.

When I saw her from across the room, my natural instinct took over at first. The pattern of acting appreciative and complimentary, but hiding my true reaction, was ingrained deeply.

But I don't have to do that anymore.

Dawn's black dress fit snugly over her hourglass figure. It showed her bare shoulders, which made me ache to stroke my fingers over them. She'd straightened the slight curl in her black hair, so it fell to her shoulders in a glossy sheet. Running my fingers through it was the least of what I wanted to do. Her makeup was subtle and only enhanced what she'd been gifted naturally. She stared at me, chin raised, her eyes daring me to react to her.

A dare I accepted readily.

Marching across the room, I pinned her with my eyes, refusing to let her gaze wander. I grasped both of her wrists and walked her backward until she butted up against the wall. Raising both hands over her head, I lowered my lips to hers. Our fingers interlaced, and a small moan escaped from deep within her as our kiss deepened.

Eventually, I stepped back after a light nip on her bottom lip. Remaining inches away, I brushed my nose over her neck, inhaling her intoxicating scent. "You look incredible. Where have you been hiding that dress all week?"

She slowly sucked the lip I'd bitten between her teeth, drawing my eye like a moth to the flame. Her lips were full from my kiss. "It's been in the closet. I brought it on a whim.

This isn't exactly a *friends* kind of dress." Then she arched a brow. "Kind of like your condoms. Insurance."

I had to laugh at that. "And neither of us had any idea we'd be using our insurance on each other."

She trailed a finger on my bare skin next to the collar of my button-up shirt, and I shivered visibly. Her lips rose into a smile as she traced down one side of my chest and up the other. "You're the one who wanted to draw things out tonight. I'm just following along."

I leaned in and inhaled again. Dawn didn't normally wear perfume, but tonight she smelled deep, mysterious, and exotic.

Exhilarating.

Intoxicating.

Raising my head, I flicked my tongue in her ear and smiled as she jolted. "Let's head to the restaurant."

The soft, melodic sounds of an acoustic guitar and keyboard reached us before we entered the restaurant. The same band as last night. I caught Kirana's eye and raised both brows. She gave me a firm nod back as Dawn headed toward our usual table.

I caught her arm. "How about we dance?"

Her surprise at being stopped morphed into happiness, and she nodded. "Best offer I've had all day."

I brushed my fingers slowly down her arm and smiled at the goose bumps rising. "I haven't even started yet."

Grasping her hand, I led her to the small dance floor, stopping a distance from another couple already dancing. I placed one hand on the small of Dawn's back and enfolded her hand with the other.

Dawn stepped close. "Have we ever danced before?"

"Not that I can recall. This is a trip for firsts, remember?"

"How could I forget?"

We settled into a slow, swaying motion. I could hardly believe I was dancing with her right now. No one would ever confuse me with a professional, but I could hold my own.

Her gorgeous lips widened into a smile as she bent her neck back to watch me. "I can really tell the differences in our heights. I've never been one to wear high heels, but I think some might be in my future."

I shook my head and brushed a kiss against her temple. "You don't have to do that. You're perfect as you are."

"Easy for you to say. You're not the one getting a kink in your neck."

I laughed as she let go of my hand, sliding her arms around my neck.

I settled mine on her hips, momentarily pressing her against me. "I think we fit together perfectly."

She brushed her fingers over my shoulders. "I'm only giving you a hard time. I love the fact that you're so tall. I've always thought of you as the guy who could have any woman he wanted, so I'm kind of amazed you've wanted *me* all these years."

I came to a complete stop, staring at her. "What? Trust me, you're all I've ever wanted. And it's not like women were beating my door down, you know."

Oh, shit. Why did I say that?

Dawn was far too perceptive to let that comment pass. "Oh, so I'm what was left at the bottom of your coffee cup, huh? A pity... relationship?"

She carefully enunciated the word, letting me know what she was substituting it for. Heat rushed across my face. Me and my damn mouth! "I didn't mean it that way! Dawn, you don't understand how long I've—"

She rose to her toes and stopped my words with a kiss, instantly calming me. When she pulled back, she was smiling. "I was teasing you. But I meant what I said. You could have any woman you wanted, Cole. You're every woman's dream, and it's high time you realized that."

I shrugged. "I always thought you were out of my league. You were the pretty, popular one. I figured you saw me as that tall, awkward kid. Didn't think I'd ever outgrow that in your eyes."

Her gaze lowered, taking in my shoulders and chest. She brushed one hand down the front of my shirt before linking her fingers again behind my neck. "I've never seen you that way, Cole. The only person who felt that way was you."

"Yeah, I'm figuring that out."

"Good. Just as I'm trying to believe that I'm not a failure at life because my vision didn't come to pass."

"Maybe that was because you were meant for something better."

My breath caught in my throat as she lifted her gaze to mine. Her blue eyes held so much emotion—so much never directed at me before. Desire, belief, love. "That's what I think. I'm so lucky to have you."

"Not as lucky as I am." We continued to sway to the music, and I pulled her closer to me and rested my arms around her waist. Fortunately, Dawn didn't seem to be in any rush to start dinner.

After thirty minutes, Kirana appeared at the edge of the restaurant and gave me a deliberate nod. I smiled back at her, a delicious thrill rolling through me. I turned my gaze to the beautiful woman in my arms. "What do you say we start dinner?"

"That sounds wonderful. After not eating much today,

I'm ready for a big dinner. Normal food." With a wide smile, she unclasped her hands and turned, heading toward our table.

I caught her hand and tugged her toward the edge of the restaurant. "Then let's get going."

"Cole—where are we..." She glanced at our table, her brow lined.

I placed my arm around her waist and led her out of the restaurant. We stepped onto the path back to our bungalow. "After what you did for me last night, I wanted to reciprocate. We're having dinner at our bungalow tonight."

Her eyes widened as a delighted smile rose across her face. "That sounds absolutely perfect!"

After I unlocked the door to our courtyard, I stepped back and ushered her in ahead of me. I held my breath, not knowing what to expect. That morning, I'd told Kirana I wanted a private dinner in our bungalow and asked if they would set a table for us while we were dancing. She'd assured me they'd take care of everything.

Now it was showtime.

"Oh my God! Cole, how is this possible?"

As I entered behind Dawn, my breath rushed out in a long exhale. Relief. And a touch of wonder.

How did they accomplish this in only thirty minutes?

Two strands of bare party bulbs crisscrossed overhead from one courtyard wall to the other. Half a dozen metal lanterns were placed on the ground, and pillar candles flickered within. My breath stilled as I gazed upon the pool. Several lily pads floated, votive candles snugged tightly on top. They drifted lazily around the pool, providing a warm, romantic glow to the area.

Our patio table had been moved to the center of the courtyard. A white cloth was draped over it, and a Haven-green runner lay on top. It was adorned with two place settings, and a nearby bottle of champagne rested in an ice bucket.

Dawn turned in a slow circle, her mouth hanging open. Her eyes met mine. "You planned this?"

"The idea, yes. But the execution was all Haven." I pulled out a chair. "Have a seat, my love."

She lowered herself, and I tucked her chair in before moving to the ice bucket. The champagne was already open, the cork wedged within to hold in the fizz. I pulled it out and poured into the two flutes sitting on the table. After I sat, I raised my glass. "To an incredible trip. And to a new start. In all sorts of ways."

Dawn touched her glass to mine, the chime echoing softly in the night. Her eyes were round as she took in our surroundings. "This is the most beautiful thing I've ever seen."

"I'm glad. You deserve it."

Nearby, two sticks of incense were lit, enveloping us in their exotic scent. A small candle on the table lit Dawn's face with a soft glow, and I swallowed over the constriction in my throat.

This is real. All of it.

A knock sounded on our courtyard door and Kirana entered, balancing two plates and a pepper grinder. "Here is your first course, a Caesar salad with our homemade dressing. Pepper?"

I grinned as Dawn inspected the salad, then breathed a relieved sigh at its ordinariness.

Kirana tucked the grinder under her arm. "I'll be back soon with your entrees."

As the door snicked shut, Dawn smiled at me. "Entrees? After last night, that sounds a little ominous."

I held a hand up. "You have nothing to worry about. I promise you'll love this."

She picked up her fork and winked at me. "I already do."

I had just refilled our glasses when Kirana returned to clear our salad plates. She brought in a small round table and left two covered dishes on it. Disappearing out the door, she returned with two larger plates that she placed before us.

"Enjoy. Steak and rock lobster, caught fresh this morning."

I grinned as Dawn's face lit up.

Kirana turned back to me. "As requested, your desserts are on the small table. When you are finished with your meal, please stack your plates on the table and leave it outside on the path. Someone will pick it up. Enjoy your evening." After a pressed-hands bow, she removed our salad plates and left our courtyard, closing the door softly behind her.

Dawn picked up her fork and knife, delight written in the smile widening her mouth. "This is one of the best benefits of having a boyfriend who knows me so well. Steak and lobster!"

I smiled back, taking extra satisfaction in her casual use of the word *boyfriend*. "All your favorites. After last night, it was the least I could do. And the dessert is chocolate lava cake."

Her eyes lit up at that—Dawn adored chocolate. After slicing into her steak, she placed the morsel in her mouth. She closed her eyes and groaned in a way that made my heart speed up. "Oh my God, I don't remember the last time I had a meal this good. Lobster!" She squealed and speared a bit, dipping it in melted butter.

I sat back in my chair, my heart beating fast for another reason now. *What the hell? She hasn't had a good meal in forever?* "Uh, don't you go out for dinner?"

She swallowed and smacked her lips. "Not nice ones. Even before the divorce, a fancy dinner was pretty unusual."

I used my knife to stab my steak, scraping the plate with a screech. With a deep breath, I set the utensils down and lifted my eyes to hers. "I should probably tell you. If Blake and I ever come face-to-face again, I'm going to pound him into the ground."

I meant every word, but I wasn't sure how Dawn would react. She whipped her head up, her eyes becoming round. Yeah, she hadn't expected that. I was a pretty mild guy.

Until I wasn't.

Her mouth moved. A small side-to-side wiggle, then it blossomed into a smile, and she leaned forward in her chair. "So, you're going to protect my honor, huh?"

I didn't smile back but tapped my index finger on the table, emphasizing my words. "Every minute of every day. That bastard didn't treat you right." And I'd only realized how much that was true on this trip.

Her eyes softened, becoming glittery. "I think my life is changing a whole lot for the better."

"It will if I have anything to say about it." I raised my champagne flute. "I'm Scarecrow. I protect what's important, remember?"

The chocolate cake was as delectable as the rest of the meal. All evening, my eye had been drawn to the pool and its floating candles. Gentle, flickering light meandered around the surface as the pump ran a current around the pool.

After swallowing my final bite of dessert, I placed the

fork on my plate and pushed it away. Piling our dishes on the small table, I placed everything on the path for the staff to pick up. Then I hung the Do Not Disturb sign on the courtyard door, closing it behind me.

Sliding back into my chair, I drained the last of my champagne. "You want to go for a swim? I think that pool is calling our name."

Her gaze drifted to the water, the candles reflecting in her eyes. She gave a dreamy sigh. "It certainly is. Hold on a second, and I'll go change into a swimsuit."

As she started to rise, I grabbed her wrist, stilling her movement. My eyes met hers and held them steady. "Who said anything about swimsuits?"

She turned her wrist, and I loosened my hold. She stroked my palm. "A little late-night skinny dipping in our private pool? You're full of good ideas tonight."

I pushed to my feet and took a strong step toward her. Surprise widened her eyes as she stepped back momentarily. Then she steadied, moving both hands to my chest. Her touch was light and delicate, yet it sent heat rushing through me. Encircling her in my arms, I lowered my head. Our lips met in a long, slow kiss. She tasted of champagne and chocolate ambrosia.

I brushed the fingers of my right hand up her back, stopping to caress her bare shoulders. Deepening the kiss, I unzipped her dress.

Chapter Twenty-Three

Cole

THE TWO SIDES of Dawn's dress parted in one fluid motion. I moved back a step and let the fabric fall to the ground. Underneath, she wore a black strapless lace bra and very skimpy black panties. My heart almost stopped cold at the sight before carrying on at a gallop. Stepping forward again, I ran my hands over her hips. Then I slowed as my fingers reached the velvety skin of her bare cheeks. I laughed softly in her ear. "I had no idea you wore thongs."

"Maybe you don't know as much about me as you thought." She unbuttoned my shirt, then ran her fingers over my chest. Her touch ignited me as she pushed my shirt over my shoulders and let it fall to the ground.

"I look forward to discovering your secrets." I trailed a line of kisses over her jaw as I softly caressed the lace fabric on the front of her panties.

She inhaled sharply through her nose. I moved to her mouth, kissing her hard.

Claiming her. After what we had been through, I needed to know she was mine. And I was hers.

Dawn stepped forward and pressed the length of her body to mine, kissing me back just as hard. Our teeth crashed together. I got her bra off in a second and cupped both breasts as she opened my slacks. Raw, hot desire pulsed through me when she slipped her hand inside and took hold of me.

My chest was already heaving with the force of my breaths, and I stepped back. "We better slow down, or we'll never make it to the pool."

I pushed my pants and underwear off as she teased her thong down her legs, keeping her eyes on me the whole time. It was the most arousing thing I'd ever seen—the knowledge that she had this hidden side.

Taking her hand, I led her to the shallow end of the pool, entering between the two loungers sitting in the water. I stepped off the shallow ledge and into the deeper, four-foot-deep section. As I turned around and gathered Dawn into my arms, a lily pad floated by, the candlelight reflecting on her face. Her sharp cheekbones shimmered in the soft light, and her lips were swollen from my kisses.

Not as swollen as they're going to be.

She ran her fingers back and forth over my upper chest, then softly drew her nails down my pecs. I jerked in a breath, arousal throbbing through me now. Meeting my eyes, she gave me a slightly bashful smile. "I have a small confession. I bought that thong specifically for this trip—I've never worn one before. Not sure I really like it, but it made me feel pretty sexy."

I kissed the tip of her nose. "Because you are the sexiest thing on the planet."

Her smile grew more confident, and she lifted onto her

tiptoes to kiss me. Opening her mouth, she slid her tongue over my lips. A whole-body jolt ran through me right before she pulled away sharply. With a sweep of her arms, she moved backward in the water, peaking a brow at me.

I laughed, launching myself after her. The motion sent ripples over the water and caused the candles to dip on their lily pads. Shadows danced across the walls of our courtyard as I pulled her tightly to me. "Want to play, huh?"

"Swimming was your idea, remember?"

As our lips came together again, she hopped up and wrapped her legs around my waist. I growled as I moved my hands to support her, and the sound increased when she ground against me. "God, you turn me on, Dawn," I said against her lips.

She pulled back to stare at me, slowly drawing one finger across my chin. "I feel so comfortable with you. You make me feel... confident."

"Good. That's how it should be." I kissed her again, probing softly with my tongue as she rubbed her breasts against my chest. I was still afraid this was all a dream and I'd wake up in my apartment at home, alone.

But it wasn't a dream. A soft half-moon watched over us, adding its light to the candles floating by.

I sucked her bottom lip into my mouth, then let go. "I want you to be comfortable. Do you want to stay out here or go inside?"

Her smile started out small but grew in size and slyness. "Well, if this is going to be anything like the other night, we better go inside. Don't want to wake up the whole resort."

I nibbled her earlobe. "As you wish."

She started to bring her legs down when I gripped her tightly, preventing her. I kissed her hard as I walked toward the pool exit.

Dawn relaxed in my arms. "You're going to carry me inside?"

I stepped onto the shallow shelf and walked between the loungers. "Yes, I am. Do you have a problem with that?"

She threw her head back and laughed. "None whatsoever. I've never been carried before." Then she tipped forward and pressed a hot, wet kiss against my neck. "You're making all my fantasies come true."

"That's my deepest desire. And this is only the beginning." The stone pavers were cool beneath my wet feet as I carried her across the courtyard. She was light in my arms, and I easily shifted her position to open the door to our bungalow.

I closed it behind me and set her on her feet. Clasping her face in both hands, I kissed her again, this time urgently. The sound of it was wet and loud inside the silent room, turning me on even more.

Dawn took my hand and led me across the room. She parted the mosquito net and the fragrant scent of roses drifted out. Red rose petals were scattered over the comforter. Closing her eyes, she took a deep breath. "Oh, this just gets better and better."

Tossing back the white comforter, she slid under it and made room for me to join her. I rolled on top, resting my weight on one elbow. She was so tiny compared to me, yet we fit together perfectly.

Like we were meant to be.

Her skin was warm and soft as I trailed my hand over her hip and side. I cupped her breast, brushing in a circle with my thumb. "You are so gorgeous. Can you tell what you do to me?" I pressed hard against her, so there could be no doubt.

Dawn made an urgent noise in her throat, half groan

and half exhalation. "Oh my God, Cole." Moving both hands to my chest, she pushed hard, rolling me over. She climbed on top, stretching out on top of me.

I ran both hands through the strands of her silky hair as I nipped, licked, and sucked at her lips. "I've wanted this for so long... wanted *you* for so long."

Without warning, she sat up, straddling me. With a featherlight touch, she traced her fingers across my chest and over my abs. I was aching now, my pulse pounding in my ears. She studied me, watching her hands as they trailed over my skin. "You are the most magnificent man. Don't ever doubt that, Cole. Ever."

Our eyes locked and I saw the truth in hers. I wasn't a bullied, skinny, awkward kid. I was a goddamn six-foot-four Olympic gold medalist. With a smile widening my lips, I simply nodded back at her.

Dawn folded over, running her tongue over my chest. "I can't believe I get to do this anytime I want."

"You'll get no argument from me."

With a light laugh, she swirled her tongue down my torso, past my navel. I loved that we could be passionate and still joke. Nothing was better than this.

But when she enveloped my shaft in her mouth, I knew I was wrong.

Okay, this is definitely better.

I tossed my arm over my eyes, giving myself over to the deep, throbbing waves overtaking me. My hips began moving rhythmically, my breath moving in tandem. She was so good at this! Which reminded me of her confession the other night.

I sat up, lifting her with me, and pressed her onto her back.

"Cole... what?"

"My turn." I pushed her knees apart and rolled my tongue around the inside of one.

She gasped, and her entire leg twitched. "You don't have to..."

Slowly, I slid both hands up her inner thighs. She arched her back as I barely brushed her sex with my thumbs. "Do you want me to stop?"

"Oh my God, no!"

"Then be quiet and let me enjoy myself." Without another word, I pressed her legs farther apart and dove in. She screamed my name as I took a long swipe with my tongue, and it damn near sent me over the edge.

Well, that would be embarrassing.

She turned me on like nothing I'd ever experienced, so I concentrated on her pleasure. And judging by how ready she was and her steadily escalating breathing, I had the same effect on her.

When she gripped my head with both knees, I tilted my gaze up to watch. Both of her eyes were closed, and she whipped her wrist to her mouth, biting it as the cries ripped out of her throat. Her entire body convulsed, eventually subsiding to twitches. Watching her, I was barely holding on.

I sat up and moved to the nightstand. Opening the condom, I moved to put it on.

"No. Let me," Dawn said softly. Her eyes were liquid in the soft light of our nightstand lamps. I handed her the condom and remained on my knees. I closed my eyes, breathing deeply as she took her time rolling it on, stroking and rubbing as she went.

When the condom was on, I pressed her onto her back and vaulted on top of her. Pushing her legs apart with my knees, I entered her with one hard thrust.

She grunted, biting my collarbone and digging her nails into my shoulders.

I recalled what she'd said about my size. I froze, watching her carefully, but her eyes were closed, a beatific smile stretching her lips. "Am I hurting you?"

"A little. Whatever you do—don't stop."

I slammed into her again, at the same time attacking her mouth. I groaned hard against her, giving her everything I had. She wrapped her legs around my waist, like she had in the pool. That brought me even closer as I rammed into her depths. "How did we not know how good we are together?" I pushed the words into her mouth, punctuated with each thrust.

Dawn didn't reply, just took my lip between her teeth and *bit* it. The confidence of the action, the bare, naked passion of it, sent my climax rolling over me. Moving both hands to her ass, I gripped her hard as I buried myself in her, giving every last part of me.

It took some time to recover, and I couldn't speak yet. I was jerking all over. Dawn traced her hands over my shoulders. When her light touch reached my lower back, it brought on another round of twitching. She laughed softly in my ear. "Oh, my love. It may have taken time to discover what we are together, but we have so much to look forward to."

Finally, I got myself together enough to roll onto one elbow. I rested my head in my hand and stared at her. "Whatever that future brings, we are both enough. You're perfect exactly as you are. Dawn, *you* are enough. Always."

She stroked my damp hair, her smile lingering. "I know."

THE NEXT MORNING, we ate breakfast and were ready to check out by 10:00 a.m. As we left the bungalow, I traced my finger over the wooden sign on our courtyard door, which read *Damai*. A smile rose on my face.

It certainly brought us peace. We worked through the strife, and look at us now.

I tried to be chivalrous and pay the bill myself, but Dawn wouldn't hear of it, insisting we split it evenly. Both of us were amazed at what a bargain Haven turned out to be. Monica, the yoga instructor, happened to be in the lobby and Dawn gave her a big hug. The older woman surprised me by giving me one too, evidently thrilled to see us together.

The trip came to a perfect full circle when our driver appeared and ushered us into the clean white SUV. Both front doors were stenciled with Haven and its stylized lotus flower. As he held the door open, I smiled at the same man Dawn and I had met in the arrival line when we first arrived in Bali.

We pulled onto the highway and not a single cloud dared to hover over the Island of the Gods. Majestic Mt. Agung stood as a sentinel, and I took time to memorize my last glimpse of it.

As we drove through the organized chaos of traffic, the driver smiled at us in the rearview mirror. "Did you enjoy your vacation? Was Bali everything you were looking for?"

I glanced at Dawn and took her hand, intertwining our fingers. She smiled at me—we had the same thoughts. I met the driver's eyes in the mirror. "Enjoy doesn't begin to describe it. We found everything we've ever wanted."

Chapter Twenty-Four

Dawn

SIX MONTHS LATER

"I'm no good with scissors, Miss Hammond." Five-year-old Kaiden turned a pair of giant, imploring blue eyes to me as he held up the piece of misshapen paper.

Heart melting, I leaned over his small desk. "You're doing great! Why don't I help you with the last bit?" I didn't blame him for having problems using the blunt safety scissors, but handing out the normal variety wasn't an option with kindergartners.

He nodded and handed me the piece of folded red construction paper. I re-cut the heart he'd attempted, managing to finish with an object that actually looked like a heart when I unfolded the paper. He lit up as I handed it back.

"Now, use this one as a guide when you cut the pink paper."

I continued around the room where my students were having varying degrees of success cutting out their Valentine's Day hearts. A pile of red, pink, and white paper rectangles lay on each child's desk. "When you finish the hearts, start making your chain. Tape the end of the paper together and join the next link as you go."

From the moment I started back at work after returning from Bali, I could feel the difference. The difference in me. I had a new appreciation for what I could offer these children and what they could offer me. All because of Cole and the certainty I carried around inside my heart now.

That I was enough.

A month after we'd come back, Cole confessed he'd run into Blake one afternoon. I'd grabbed his hand and checked his knuckles carefully, but no punches had been thrown.

Cole shrugged. "Blake wasn't worth the effort." The gleam in his eye told me he'd gotten some choice words in, though. Then Cole smiled. "Besides, he's a loser. I'm a three-time gold medalist."

I cocked my head, puzzled until the piece fell into place and a wide smile nearly cracked my face. The third gold medal he referred to was me.

Us.

Across the classroom, six-year-old Daisy held up three links in triumph. "Look, Miss Hammond! I did it."

I applauded her and continued my rounds, giving extra encouragement to less successful kids.

Half an hour later, Dana Proctor, a mother who volunteered regularly, helped me link the various chains into two long ones. Standing on opposite sides of the room, we hung them above the students. As I taped my streamer to the wall, the class bell rang, sending the kids into a tizzy of activity.

"See you tomorrow!" I shouted with a laugh. "And don't forget to take the Valentine you made home to your family."

Dana joined me at my desk as the children filed out of the room. "What about you? Where's your Valentine?"

I laughed ruefully. "Cole has been working like a fiend lately. I don't think he even remembers it's Valentine's Day today. I'm going to the gym now for my training session."

Dana pouted. "That doesn't sound very romantic."

"I'm sure we'll make the most of it."

Cole and I had surprised several friends when we came back from Bali as a full-fledged couple. Others had stared at us and said, "What took you so long?"

Our parents were very happy. We quickly settled into a new routine. Mine didn't change much, but Coach Terry retired soon after we got back, and Cole threw himself into his new business.

He'd changed the name immediately, which had resulted in the loss of some clients, though I got the feeling Cole didn't mourn the loss of the cocky, cliquey few who left. Cole wanted anyone setting foot inside his facility to feel welcome and part of something special, whether they were a weekend warrior or a world-class athlete. I fully supported him, knowing that the early months of a new venture were critical.

Cole always made time for us, and we had plenty of date nights. Though I was just as happy snuggling under a blanket while we watched a movie on the couch. My relationship with him was fundamentally different than any I'd had before. I was happier, more secure, and more confident.

I didn't need a dozen roses to know he loved me.

Every day was living proof of that.

I changed into leggings and a T-shirt in the staff bathroom, then headed outside. I texted Cole as I got into my car.

Dawn: I'm on my way.

Cole: See you soon. I'm in my office.

I shook my head, smiling, and texted back.

Dawn: You can't give me a personal training session in your office!

Cole: Oh, yes I can. You have no imagination.

Dawn: Okay, now I'm hurrying.

With a laugh, I tossed my phone in the center console and drove to the gym. Despite his teasing, I had no doubt Cole would insist on a thorough weight routine today. I'd been working with him for five months and loved the muscle definition appearing all over my body.

Cole was a fan too.

The gym was only fifteen minutes from my school. I parked and turned off the engine, pride filling me as I gazed at the large sign on the wall above the door. Gold Medal Fitness was already making a name for itself, and I couldn't have been prouder of Cole when he'd announced with a shy smile what he was naming his new venture. He chose a name that exemplified who he was and was aspirational to his clients as well.

As I walked by the check-in desk, I waved at Benny, the high school kid who worked afternoons. I strolled down the hall, with offices and classrooms on each side. At the end was a T-intersection, and Cole's office was at the end of the right side.

I turned the corner and nearly stepped on something. What looked like cards were placed at even intervals on the floor leading down the hall. I bent down and picked up the one I'd nearly stepped on, and my breath stilled in my lungs.

It was the first Valentine I'd ever given Cole, one of the kinds that come in a box for children to hand out to classmates. This one was a cartoon of a puppy. A second card lay farther down. I wandered down the hallway, picking up reminders of Valentines past. I'd given him the final card his senior year in high school. Inside, I'd written, *Knock 'em dead at Texas, Scarecrow.*

A lump formed in my throat. *I guess he didn't forget after all.*

After stacking the cards in a neat pile, I held them against my heart with one hand while I opened Cole's office door with the other. He was in front of his desk, leaning back against it.

And dressed in a gray suit with a red tie, his hair sharply styled.

I burst into laughter as I shut the door behind me. "I am definitely underdressed for this workout." I slid up to him and pulled his head down to mine.

We settled into a long and delicious kiss. I didn't want it to end.

Eventually, he pulled back to smile seductively at me. "You look perfect to me."

I held up the Valentines, then clutched them to my chest again. "You saved these? This is the sweetest Valentine's gift I've ever received."

"Glad you like it. I only save Valentines from the most important people, and you're number one on that list."

I pressed my lips to his again, then murmured in his ear, "Thank you. I have a little present for you too, but it's in my lingerie drawer. I'll show it to you later."

He made an appreciative noise deep in his throat and nuzzled my ear. "Hold on to that thought."

I lowered my eyes to his desktop. A heart-shaped box of chocolates lay on it, drawing a laugh out of me. "Are chocolates part of our training session?"

He arched a brow. "What's the point of working out if you can't enjoy yourself once in a while?"

"I agree completely. Especially when it involves chocolate." Plus, the box was from a nearby artisan candy maker. I couldn't wait to see what was inside—my mouth already watered.

Cole smiled as he reached to grab the box. "I've known you for a long time, and I know better than to get between you and chocolate. You can have the first choice."

Balancing the box in one hand, he removed the lid and set it on the desk. Then he presented the heart-shaped box to me. I rubbed my hands together, already tasting the deliciousness.

The box was full of dark, milk, and white chocolates of every shape, some with frosting added. Gleefully, I inspected the individual pieces in their shallow molds. Then my gaze caught, and I needed a moment to understand what I saw.

One cell was different.

The one with a diamond ring nestled inside.

I froze, both hands flying to cover my mouth. As my heart threatened to burst from my chest, I lifted my eyes to Cole's.

With a small smile lifting one side of his mouth, he plucked the ring out, setting the box on top of the lid. He moved in front of me and lowered to one knee, smoothing his red tie and suit jacket. Then he lifted his hands and presented the ring. "Dawn Hammond, will you marry me?"

Euphoric tears filled my eyes. I started nodding before I was even aware of it. Then I rushed my hands down. "Yes! Absolutely, one hundred percent. Yes!"

His smile grew as he pushed to his full height. He grasped my left hand and slid the ring onto my third finger. Made of white gold, the prominent solitaire was surrounded by a halo of smaller stones.

It was breathtaking, the most beautiful ring I'd ever seen.

Cole placed a knuckle under my chin, wrenching my gaze away as he lifted my face. Our eyes held. Folding my hand within his, he leaned down and brushed a soft kiss over my lips. "I love you, Pooh-Bear."

My tears ran over as a laugh tumbled out of my mouth. His proposal was perfect. Everything about Cole was perfect, and I couldn't wait to be his wife. "I love you too, Scarecrow. Let's get married."

Epilogue

Cole

SIX MONTHS LATER

As Dawn and I swam over the shallow reef, an enormous school of yellow-tail snappers split around us. Surrounded by shimmering yellow, we exchanged grins. The experience brought back memories of Bali, though this time we were closer to home. And that wasn't the only difference. I smiled at the ring on my left hand.

Our second beach vacation was almost exactly one year after Bali. We'd kept in touch with Quinn and Steph, who had sent a generous gift for our wedding in April, though they couldn't attend the ceremony in person. Dawn and I couldn't wait to start our lives together, so we arranged a simple wedding in a local arboretum two months after I proposed.

We lived in a rented bungalow near her school and

Gold Medal Fitness. It wasn't fancy, but the low rent allowed us to focus on making the gym a success. I had big ambitions for my gym and would love to add a competition pool at some point. But that would be a very expensive proposition. We both wanted our own home, but that purchase would have to wait until later.

Dawn had already been one of the more popular teachers in her school, but her spirit was renewed while in Bali and it showed. She was back attending online classes for her master's degree and couldn't wait to go to work every morning. Many parents were requesting her for the upcoming school year, and several of her kindergartners cried on the last day of school.

Early in the summer, Steph had contacted Dawn, raving about her and Quinn's visit to Half Moon Bay Resort. Insisting it would be perfect for us.

And here we were. Underwater again.

Granted, we were snorkeling over the reef, not diving. But I wasn't complaining, especially since we were getting a guided tour of Half Moon Bay's house reef from the head dive guide himself. Alex Monroe was the only one of the three of us not wearing a snorkel. Apparently, he didn't need it. During our tour, he often swam submerged for several minutes before needing a breath.

Alex finned gracefully in front of us, finding multitudes of creatures in the crannies and crevices of the reef. I was astonished by how much he saw—animals invisible to my inexperienced eyes. I'd thought Quinn and Wayan were good in the water, but Alex was next-level, moving through the water like he was part fish.

He continued, swooping over a protruding edge of reef, then stilled. Alex tilted his head, fixated on something. Whipping his head around, he beckoned to us, waving his hand rapidly for us to hurry. He gave us the hand signal for octopus, which got my heart hammering. Dawn and I eagerly approached, and I took her hand as the pale blue creature slid onto a coral outcropping. It spread over the top, blanketing the surface. In an instant, the octopus turned a mottled brown, matching its surroundings, and developed stubby protrusions over its mantle.

I gasped, the sound loud as I exhaled through my snorkel. Alex grinned at me, his vivid blue eyes sparkling behind his mask. We watched the octopus for several minutes as it sinuously moved from coral head to coral head before finally disappearing into an impossibly small crevice.

When we reached waist-deep water, we removed our fins. "Thanks for the tour," I said to Alex. "I imagine you'd rather be leading divers."

The man laughed, ruffling his sandy hair as he shrugged. His age was difficult to guess. He was very fit and looked in his mid-thirties. "You did me a favor. I was supposed to do inventory this afternoon. I'd *much* rather be here."

Dawn clasped my forearm. "Cole, you can go on tomorrow's dive. Just because I can't dive doesn't mean you have to skip it."

I glanced at her and shook my head. "No, snorkeling is great. We'll dive again in the future. We've got plenty of other things to do on the island."

We stepped out of the ocean onto a powdery white-sand beach with a line of palm trees swaying in the gentle breeze. An attractive woman slightly older than us approached. Wearing a staff T-shirt and black capris, her chestnut-colored hair was pulled into a ponytail. We'd met resort owner Hope Collins at a reception the previous evening.

She greeted all three of us with a smile, her gaze

lingering on Alex for a moment longer. "How was the snorkeling adventure?"

"Wonderful!" Dawn said. "The water is so clear and warm, and Alex gave us a great tour. We saw so much!" She passed her slightly dazed eyes over the blinding sand. "I've never seen sand this white. After some beach time tomorrow, we're going to Christiansted to poke around."

"Excellent," Hope replied. "There's plenty to see. Don't miss the Danish fort."

The previous evening, Hope had provided an open bar at the manager's reception. I'd enjoyed a glass of wine, feeling slightly guilty when I glanced at Dawn's soft drink. Even Alex showed up—that was when we set up our snorkeling trip. We'd been surprised but pleased when he'd offered to guide us at no charge.

Now, as the sun caressed our shoulders, Hope turned her gaze to Alex, eyeing him with a slight smile. "Oh—no snorkeling tomorrow, huh? Poor Alex. You'll have to come up with a fresh excuse to delay inventory."

Alex grinned back. "Don't worry. I'll work on one."

"You can't avoid it forever."

I laughed, now understanding what he'd been up to, and happy we were part of it.

Alex folded his arms, beads of saltwater tumbling down his muscular chest, then turned his smile to us. "Boss Lady runs a tight ship. She likes to crack the whip on me."

Hope's eyes darted back to him at that last comment, and she arched a brow. Alex met her gaze, a definite challenge glinting in his eyes. A strong current passed between them—the air felt almost electric.

Finally, Hope slid her eyes to Dawn. "My recalcitrant dive guide isn't actually the reason I'm here." Alex's smile grew, but she pointedly ignored him. "I've got everything set up for your private dinner tonight. Do you want to have it on your deck, so you can watch the sunset?"

I turned to Dawn and smiled. "I can't think of anything better."

"Me neither," Dawn replied, shifting her gaze to Hope. "Our deck would be fabulous."

"Perfect. We'll take care of everything. Enjoy your afternoon."

As we headed toward our bungalow, Hope and Alex strolled side by side toward the resort complex of buildings and a long pier jutting into the ocean. Alex leaned down and said something to her. Hope tipped her head back and laughed, their shoulders brushing as they walked.

Dawn cocked her head as the pair retreated. "Are those two a couple? I can't figure them out."

I shrugged and draped my arm over her shoulders, stroking my finger over her silky skin. "Dunno. Never thought about it."

"I watched them last night at the reception. Some serious signals were going back and forth between those two. And again, just now."

I leaned down and nuzzled her ear as we climbed up the steps of our beach bungalow. The temperature cooled as we stepped onto the covered porch. "Maybe they're like us and trying to be professional when people are watching." I eyed the table for two, which would become our romantic dinner table tonight, then laughed. "I wish them good luck—I'm not sure how successful we are anytime you walk into the gym. My mind kind of goes out the window."

Dawn smiled back and tilted her wrist to look at her watch. "We've got a couple of hours before dinner. I'm going to take a little nap."

I came to a halt, my hand clasping her shoulder. "Are you feeling okay?"

She patted my bicep and gave me a tolerant smile. My question was a frequent one. "Doing fine, Dad. I just get tired more easily. Besides, what's the point of vacations if you can't take a nap when you want to?"

"Can't argue with that." I whisked my lips over hers, still in awe that I was kissing Dawn—my *wife*—in a Caribbean paradise. And we were going to become parents.

Before our intimate April wedding, Dawn had still been concerned about her ability to become pregnant. After assuring her I was willing to leave the situation up to fate, we agreed to wait six months before seeing a specialist.

Dawn's pregnancy test had been positive on our three-month anniversary. Her doctor assured us that she was a very healthy pregnant woman, and the baby was growing exactly as it should. On Quinn and Steph's advice, we hastily arranged this honeymoon, since we likely wouldn't be going anywhere after the baby was born.

Through the window, I watched Dawn lie down on the king-sized bed. It faced the ocean behind me, and she smiled back at me before turning on her side and closing her eyes.

As elated as I was at the prospect of becoming a father, Dawn's pregnancy had a much deeper meaning for me. She'd been instrumental in helping me reach my greatest goal. Now I was doing the same for her. And now her dream was becoming mine.

Two hours later, we sat on our bungalow deck. A white-and-aqua tablecloth draped over our table for two, place settings ready for the evening. Half Moon Bay Resort was on the western edge of St. Croix, and the bungalows all boasted outstanding views of the ocean.

And the sunset, which had been spectacular half an hour ago.

Now, as the day faded, the sky was lit in shades of lavender, pink, red, and other colors I couldn't name. We both ordered the fresh catch, blackened, and it was one of the most delicious meals I'd ever tasted. The seasoning was fiery and yet subtle, enhancing the flaky fish without over-powering it.

I took a sip of my Leatherback beer and sighed. "As wonderful as Bali was, this place has a peaceful vibe that's completely different."

Dawn nodded as she studied the resort restaurant and pool distantly visible. "I can see why Steph and Quinn raved about it so much. It's as quiet or busy as you want it to be. We might have to make this a regular trip. When we're not knee deep in babies, anyway."

I smiled and took her hand. "We'll bring them with us. I've seen a couple of kids here." The resort was very inti-mate with only eight bungalows. Though designed to attract couples, a family with young children was vaca-tioning here also.

Dawn laughed and sipped her water. "I can't believe how things have changed. Bali was the fulcrum that shifted our lives. Now we're on the best course imaginable."

Emotion welled from deep within me, and I squeezed her hand, needing to touch her. I never wanted to stop touching her. "It helped us realize what we were always meant to have. Each other."

She ran her hand over her still-flat stomach and lifted her eyes to mine. "Not just each other anymore."

I swallowed thickly, needing to clear my throat. "No. And that's the best thing of all."

———

I HOPE you loved Dawn and Cole's story! I absolutely loved writing this book—Bali is very near and dear to my heart. So many details in this book were taken from my own travels, including the pig alongside the road and the child riding the one wheeled-bike. And yes, the females porters of Tulamben are real too!

And readers who have been with me for a while might have been drumming their feet with happiness at seeing Hope and Alex again. I couldn't resist...

Next, the Island Escapes series moves onto a new exotic destination, this one in the Florida Keys. Calypso Key is almost one of the main characters in BETTING ON PARADISE, a friends to lovers, fake relationship billionaire romance. My long time readers might recognize the setting and some of the cameos...

BETTING ON PARADISE
Coming May, 2025!

From hockey hero to tabloid trainwreck, I'm betting everything on a fake romance in paradise—with very real stakes.

Nate:

I'm a former NHL star now skating on thin ice, and one scandal away from losing it all. My brother's ultimatum is clear—clean up my act or kiss my stake in our billion-dollar sports betting empire goodbye. The solution? A fake-relationship vacation in the Florida Keys to rehab my image.

Enter Camille Sullivan, my childhood friend and girl next door. In sultry Calypso Key, each staged dinner and public touch is for show. Until sun-soaked days blur into sizzling nights, and the heat between us becomes very real.

Camille peels away my layers, daring me to reveal who I really am. My heart is on the line, and she holds all the cards. As fake and real love blur, I face my biggest gamble. Will my past mistakes cost me the only woman who's ever truly known me In this high-stakes game of love, we're both playing with fire.

Betting on Paradise is part of the Island Escapes series of interconnected standalones. This billionaire fake relationship, friends to lovers steamy beach read will have you swooning for Nate and Camille.!

BETTING ON PARADISE
Coming May, 2025!

I HAVE an extra offer for you. If you'd like a glimpse into Dawn and Cole's happily ever after, be sure to sign up for my Beach Read Update.

As a thank you, **I'll send you a bonus scene** that peeks into their lives several years in the future. Click below to sign up:

Beach Read Update
(www.erinbrockus.com/bib)

Because of You: A Small Town Fake Relationship Romance

Memories of You: A Small Town Second Chance Romance

Shades of You: A Small Town Forbidden Romance

ASSOCIATED SHORT STORIES AND NOVELLAS:

Traces of You: A Small Town Rivals to Lovers Romance*

* Subscriber exclusive

HALF MOON BAY SERIES:

MAIN NOVELS:

Finding Hope: Half Moon Bay Book 1

Defending Hope: Half Moon Bay Book 2

Rising Hope: Half Moon Bay Book 3

Forever Hope: Half Moon Bay Book 4

Half Moon Whim: Half Moon Bay Book 5 (Standalone)

Half Moon Ember: Half Moon Bay Book 6 (Standalone)

Half Moon Aqua: Half Moon Bay Book 7

Crowning Hope: Half Moon Bay Book 8

The Half Moon Bay Collection Books 1-4: The Hope and Alex
Story

Associated Short Stories and Novellas:

Tropical Dawn: A Half Moon Bay Prequel Novella

*Tropical Chance**: A Second Chance Half Moon Bay Novella

*Tropical Hope**: A Half Moon Bay Prequel Short Story

* Subscriber exclusives

Dive into steamy small-town romance, where passion meets paradise!

Award-winning author Erin Brockus writes steamy small town romances that transport readers to exotic, tropical destinations, and provide a perfect beachy getaway from everyday life. Her mature, relatable characters are impossible not to root for, and she weaves breezy romantic adventure into her stories, emphasizing scuba diving and the ocean.

Drawing on her twin passions for diving and travel, Erin infuses her characters and narratives with a sense of excitement and passion. Her idea of the perfect day involves sipping a cocktail on the beach after exploring the ocean depths.

Erin lives in Washington wine country with her husband, who is also a scuba instructor. She is currently hard at work on her next island adventure. When she's not writing, you might find her out for a run or cycling through the countryside on the next quest for adventure.